Praise for Tracy Wolff!

"Wolff does an amazing job depicting Rhiannon's fear and insecurity, as well as Shawn's desire to help her get over both."
—*RT Book Reviews* on *Unguarded*

"*The Christmas Present* is more traditional in its plot (lovers from the opposites sides of the track) but the characterization is...strong."
—*Dear Author* on *The Christmas Present*

"*Unguarded* is a deeply compelling, character driven novel."
—*Lynette's Two Cents* on *Unguarded*

"Wolff is an excellent writer."
—*IReadRomance.com* on *The Christmas Wedding*

Dear Reader,

I am so excited that *Healing Dr. Alexander* has finally made it to the shelves. This is my second book about doctors working to make the world a better place. Jack's story has haunted me for years and I'm thrilled to have this chance to share it with the world.

I first got the idea for these books—and this story, in particular—when I was still in graduate school. Though I knew I wasn't ready to write it then (too busy juggling school, teaching and a new baby) it was an idea I couldn't let go of. So I filed it away, and when it came time to propose my latest ideas to Harlequin, I knew it was finally time for me to write this book.

Healing Dr. Alexander is a story of love and redemption, preconceived notions and second chances. My main characters, Jack and Sophie, have both had a really difficult time of it in recent years and I love the fact that, despite all their pain, mistrust and determination to go it alone, in the end they find their way to each other and their happily-ever-after. It isn't an easy road—with their pasts and their baggage, trusting in something as nebulous as love is about as easy as going for a root canal without anesthetic. But somehow they manage it, and I'm so glad they do. Putting the end on this story and giving these two the future they both richly deserve was one of the most satisfying things I've done in a very long time. I hope, when you get to the end, you'll agree.

Thanks so much for picking up *Healing Dr. Alexander* and giving Jack and Sophie a chance. I love hearing from my readers via email at tracy@tracywolff.com or on my blog, www.tracywolff.blogspot.com.

Happy reading,

Tracy Wolff

Healing
Dr. Alexander
Tracy Wolff

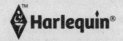

TORONTO NEW YORK LONDON
AMSTERDAM PARIS SYDNEY HAMBURG
STOCKHOLM ATHENS TOKYO MILAN MADRID
PRAGUE WARSAW BUDAPEST AUCKLAND

Recycling programs
for this product may
not exist in your area.

ISBN-13: 978-0-373-71781-1

HEALING DR. ALEXANDER

Copyright © 2012 by Tracy L. Deebs-Elkenaney

ABOUT THE AUTHOR

Tracy Wolff collects books, English degrees and lipsticks, and has been known to forget where—and sometimes who—she is when immersed in a great novel. At six, she wrote her first short story—something with a rainbow and a prince—and at seven, she ventured into the wonderful world of girls' lit with her first Judy Blume novel. By ten, she'd read everything in the young-adult and classics sections of her local bookstore, so in desperation her mom started her on romance novels. And from the first page of the first book, Tracy knew she'd found her lifelong love. Tracy lives in Texas with her husband and three sons, where she pens romance novels and teaches writing at her local community college.

Books by Tracy Wolff

HARLEQUIN SUPERROMANCE

For my husband.

Love,
Tracy

PROLOGUE

"DR. ALEXANDER, now!"

The panic in the head nurse's voice barely penetrated Jack Alexander's concentration as he searched for the bleeder that, if not stopped, would claim his patient's life. The top of the damn artery had started to roll back up the leg and he was having a difficult time finding it amidst all the blood.

"Dr. Alexander!" Becca's shrill voice called his name a second time.

"Whatever it is, it's going to have to wait!" he said, not taking his eyes from the teenage boy on the gurney in front of him. "I've only got a couple of minutes here or I'm going to lose him."

The clinic didn't have enough blood stored to make up for what was currently being pumped out of the poor kid. And while there was a line of people hundreds deep outside the clinic, most of the Somali patients were too close to starvation to afford the blood loss that came with donating. No, if this boy had any chance of survival at all, Jack had to find the top half of the shorn artery. Now.

"They want to talk to whoever's in charge. I told them you were in surgery. They didn't care."

"Who?" he asked, distractedly. Then turning to Ruth, the nurse who was assisting him, he barked, "Stretch his leg out as far as you can. I've got to dig for it." It was times like these that he missed his fully equipped operating room back in the States. Performing surgery in an ill-equipped tent in Somalia might have been his calling, but in moments like this it was also a horror.

"The Shahab," Becca told him, her voice low and urgent and frightened. That got his attention.

"They're here?" he demanded, even as he dug deeper into his patient's leg. He was deadly aware of the moments that kept ticking by. In another ninety seconds this whole situation was going to be moot because the teenager on the table in front of him would be dead. Damn it. He glanced down at the kid's face. He couldn't have been more than fourteen or fifteen. Far too young to die.

"They're outside. They want supplies."

"We just gave them stuff last week," he said, following the path the artery had taken, his gloved fingers slipping. Thank God they'd had enough anesthesia to knock the kid out—this time. But if they gave the Somali warlords any more supplies, they wouldn't have enough for the next emergency. The next shipment from For the Children wasn't expected for at least three more weeks. "Tell them we don't have anything left to share."

"I did. They aren't listening."

The panic in her voice finally got through to him, but there was nothing he could do about it. Not then, as his fingers finally brushed against the ragged edge of the severed artery. "Stay here," he told her as he twisted his arm and shoved his hand a little deeper. "I'll take care of them when I'm done with this surgery."

"I don't think they're going to wait."

"They're going to have to," he snapped, "because I'm not letting this kid go." He finally got hold of the artery and pinched it tightly between his thumb and forefinger. "Get the clamp ready, Ruth."

She already had the surgical clamp in her hand, and extended toward him. He tugged on the artery, not bothering to be gentle. The boy was going to feel like hell when the anesthesia wore off, but at least now he actually had a chance of waking up. Here, now, that was all the hope Jack could offer him.

The knowledge grated his insides raw, but he couldn't afford to dwell on it. Not right now.

He finally got the artery back down where he could see it, and within seconds had it clamped off, the steady pulsing of blood finally stopped. "Okay, I need the sutures," he told Ruth. The kid was out of immediate danger, but now came the delicate process of mending the artery. "*Fin* Dr. Alexander?" he heard the gruff words behind him.

"*Am shi!*" he shouted at the rebels to get out. This might not be a sterile OR to start with, but that didn't mean he wanted them tracking in God only knew what kind of germs while his patient's leg was wide open.

Even as he yelled, he hadn't turned around. There wasn't time to be distracted. His nimble hands began weaving the ragged edges of the artery back together. "Get the last pint of O negative," he told Ruth. "We've got to get it in him, quick."

"Not so fast," said Mussa, the leader of the rebels. "Nobody gets anything until we have what we came for."

There was the unmistakable sound of a gun being cocked, and Jack finally glanced up from what he was doing in time to see his nurse's face, livid with fear. "Ruth," he told her with firm authority, refusing to let her drown in her own panic. "Go get the blood." If he could get her away from the rebels, it was one less person for them to hurt.

A gunshot rang out, slamming into the dirt floor near the foot of the hospital gurney even as he tensed for impact. "Damn it!" he shouted. "We've got oxygen going in here. You're going to blow us all up if you're not careful."

A bunch of muttered words in Arabic followed his exclamation, and then one of the soldiers—who wasn't any older than the boy he was currently working on—strode over to the table, shut off the gas that was flowing.

"What the hell are you doing?" Jack exploded, only half lunging over the table at him. The only thing that kept him from fully going after the guy was that he couldn't afford to stop working. Not now. "Turn that back on!"

There was no response. Jack's attention and his fingers flew over the torn artery, determined to finish as quickly as possible. His patient wouldn't die without the oxygen, but it wasn't optimum, either. Not like anything here was, but still… "Look, let me finish what I'm doing and then we can talk about this," he said in the most conciliatory tone he could manage. Which wasn't really, but it was better than swearing at them—or hitting them—both of which he wanted to do. Both of which might mean the difference between life and death for his patient.

The soldier pulled out a pistol, cocked it, and pointed it straight at Jack. "We want to talk now."

"I'm almost finished, damn it. If I stop now, he'll lose his leg."

The man behind him—obviously the leader—laughed. "What does it matter to me if he loses his leg? I need supplies and don't have time to waste."

Jack swore again. "Fine, Ruth and Becca will take you back. You can—" He broke off as another shot rang out, this time mere inches from his feet.

"We want you." He paused for emphasis before continuing. "Our general believes you were not as generous last time as you could have been."

Anger ripped through Jack. He'd turned over half of his supplies to the bastards the last time they'd been here, so many that he'd all but crippled the clinic. It was a bitter pill to swallow at the best of times—and this was far from the best of times. Still, the alternative was having them ransack the place, destroying whatever they didn't want. Or worse, having them make life so awful here that For the Children would have to pull out altogether. As it was, they were one of a very few relief clinics that had been allowed into the country to begin with.

While it was true the clinic could help more people if they got to keep all the supplies they received each month, at the same time, how many people would die if they weren't here to help at all? It was a trade-off that hurt him deeply, but one he'd learned to live with through the years. In this, Somalia was no different from Eritrea or Chechnya or Haiti.

Tamping down on the resentment and fury that were ravaging him from the inside, he muttered, "Fine, whatever. I'm almost done." He kept working even as he fumed. Another couple of minutes and it would be complete. The other doctor on staff could close the wound up.

"Now!" the leader said. And this time he was the one walking around the table, pointing a gun at Jack.

"Okay, okay." He was almost finished, almost—

This time when the soldier fired three times, Jack didn't even flinch, expecting the bullets to slam into the ground once again. His adrenaline was so high that it took him a full thirty seconds to comprehend that these shots hadn't been fired at the dirt. Even then he didn't understand, even then he didn't feel anything until his patient's artery began, once again, to spurt blood.

He went to stop it, tried to clamp the newly severed ends, but his fingers wouldn't respond. They wouldn't do what he needed them to do. And that's when he finally understood. They hadn't just shot his patient. They'd shot him, as well.

CHAPTER ONE

HE NEEDED TO get out of the car. Jack knew it, just as he knew his best and oldest friend, Dr. Amanda Jacobs, was waiting for him inside the run-down clinic. He'd been due to meet her here two hours ago, but somehow he'd found a million reasons to be late. Lingering over a lunch he didn't want and couldn't bring himself to eat, filling the rental car up with gas, exploring websites about sightseeing in Atlanta, though he had no desire to actually visit the place. Anything and everything to keep him from this parking lot, this moment, this decision he wasn't ready to make.

Not that it was a done deal, he reassured himself as he finally reached for the door handle. He hadn't agreed to anything. He was here to see his friend, to take a look around. Checking out the clinic didn't mean he was promising anything. To Amanda or himself. It proved he was interested in what his friend had been getting up to.

Still, the walk to the front door of the clinic was a long one. And not just because of the bowling ball in his stomach. Both his leg and his hand ached from where he'd been shot two months before; Atlanta's humidity exacerbating the still recovering tendons.

Which brought up the question he'd been asking himself ever since his plane had landed the night before. What was he doing here? His doctor was in Boston. His physical therapist was in Boston. His family was in Boston. And yet here he was, in Atlanta, checking out a clinic he had absolutely no interest in working in.

This whole trip was stupid. A joke. He didn't belong here any more than he belonged in the fancy family practice his father had gotten him an interview at in Boston last week. He hadn't been interested in that job, either, but his father had refused to take no for an answer. Dealing with sniffles and high blood pressure was a long way from being Chief of Thoracic Surgery at John Hopkins, but it was better than "scrabbling away in that pathetic little hovel in Africa," as the elder Jack Alexander liked to say.

The casual cruelty, and inherent snobbery, of his father's words was what made Jack dial up Amanda in the first place, then take her up on her frequently issued invitation to come see the newest project she was involved in.

Atlanta felt too foreign, too strange, and that was even before he took into account his ridiculous feelings for Amanda. Feelings that wouldn't go away, no matter how hopeless they were.

And they were hopeless, he reminded himself viciously. They'd been friends for well over a decade—ever since they'd met as first years at Harvard Medical School—and though he'd been in love with her since they'd duked it out for the top spot in the program, she'd never seen him as anything more than a pal. And now she was married—*married*—to another of Jack's closest buddies and any tiny hope he'd held on to that they might one day be together had been officially destroyed.

He closed his eyes, took a deep breath. Started to head to the car. No, he didn't belong here. But that was the problem, wasn't it? He didn't belong anywhere. Not anymore. Not like he used to. These days he was a shell of his former self, one who could barely hold a stethoscope steady let alone a scalpel.

Jack cut off the familiar thought as he forced himself to turn back around and step into the clinic. He let the cracked glass door with its iron burglar bars swing shut behind him. The pity party was getting old. Especially since he was the only one at the table. Sick of himself, and the grinding pain he couldn't escape no matter how many exercises he did, he tried to distract himself by looking around. Analyzing the surroundings.

There wasn't much to analyze. The waiting room was large and spare, its walls painted with what he guessed had once been cream, but was now more of a dingy yellow splashed with stains. People sat on folding chairs, crammed into every available space, while a couple of forlorn plants—ones that had definitely seen better days—sat in the front corner of the room next to a high counter. Behind it, a large, African-American woman worked on a computer, several charts stacked in front of her. It all reminded him a lot more of his tent clinic in Somalia than the private practice his family was trying to force him to join.

To the woman's left was a small sliding-glass window. There were about a dozen people lined up in front of it, all bedraggled and clearly feeling sick and miserable. Nothing compared to the patients he'd seen in Somalia, but still it was obvious these people needed help.

He felt that old familiar stirring inside of him, the one that demanded he roll up his sleeves and pitch in. This was what he did. What he was good at.

He beat the urge back down. This was what he had done. What he had been good at. These days, he could barely dress himself let alone practice medicine.

Despite the fact that the clinic was overcrowded, it was obviously efficiently run. Though the line of people was growing, they were being rapidly signed in and triaged. Behind the window, he could see a nurse taking temperatures even as she typed notes into a computer.

Not that he was surprised. Amanda could work anywhere, could practice medicine in the middle of war zones and natural disasters without blinking an eye. But she demanded efficiency of everyone around her—or at least she did when she wasn't drowning in sorrow.

Seeing the way this clinic ran like clockwork, convinced him even more that he'd made the right decision all those months ago. Getting her out of Africa so she could deal with the loss of her child and regain her health, had been exactly the right thing to do. Even if, in doing so, he had lost her forever.

The loss was bittersweet, especially now that he could see that she really had found herself again here in this run-down, little clinic in Atlanta. He'd sent her out of Somalia a year ago, so burned out and run-down he was afraid she would work herself to death. He'd told her to take a vacation. Instead, she'd ended up here.

And now, somehow, so had he.

Not that he was planning on getting involved, he assured himself. He was just here to see an old friend, to see for himself that she really was okay and to assure her the same thing about him. He'd take her and Simon to dinner later that evening. Tell a few stories, crack a few jokes, and then catch the first flight back to Massachusetts in the morning. It would be easy, so easy that even he couldn't screw it up.

Now that he had a plan, Jack straightened his shoulders.

Flexed his already cramping hand.

Made sure his I'm-in-control-and-master-of-my-own-destiny mask was firmly in place, then headed toward the front of the waiting room.

He figured his best bet was the woman behind the computer because, as he'd been standing here thinking, the line at the small window had only gotten longer. So he leaned on the high counter, hoping if he took some weight off his leg it would stop throbbing quite so badly. He smiled at the woman.

"I'm here to—"

"The line starts over there." She pointed at the window without ever looking away from the computer.

"I can see that. However, I want to talk to—"

"Over. There." The finger jabbed at the air for emphasis, but the woman still didn't look at him.

"Again. I see the window. However, I'm a friend of—"

She did look at him then, her eyebrows pulled low over her eyes and her mouth curled downward. "I don't actually care if you're friends with the surgeon general, the president of the United States and Denzel Washington. The line starts over there." Again she stabbed a finger in the direction of the window, than grunted as she reached for another file and began inputting its content into the computer.

Jack stared at her for a few moments, then turned to look at the line she was directing him to. It had grown exponentially in the past five minutes, efficient nurses or not. His leg throbbed, his hand ached and the last thing he wanted to do was to stand around for the next hour while he waited on a chance to see Amanda.

Maybe it wasn't meant to be, he told himself as he pulled his cell phone out of his pocket and flipped through his contacts until he found her cell number. He'd call Amanda and if she didn't pick up—and she probably wouldn't as she was more than likely with a patient—he'd call it a day. After all, he'd tried his best. He'd shown up, talked to the office manager, had tried to explain who he was. It wasn't his fault that she wouldn't listen.

Ignoring the voice in his head that told him he was being a coward and taking the easy way out, Jack listened to Amanda's voice mail greeting and left a brief message letting her know that he was in the waiting room. Then he headed for the door, doing his best to justify the fact that he was—despite his good intentions—running away.

He assured himself that he wasn't afraid of touring this little, low-income clinic. It was simply that he had better things to do. Like staring at the ceiling of his hotel room…

"Jack!" Amanda's voice rang through the waiting room, foiling his escape. He froze, his hand on the door handle. "Where are you going?"

He turned to see her barreling through the door that separated the waiting room from the rest of the clinic. Then she was hurtling herself into his arms and his only choice was to brace himself with his good leg and catch her or let her take them both to the floor.

"Hey! Where's the fire?" he asked, even as he wrapped his arms around her in a huge bear hug.

"I'm so glad you're here!" she said, stretching up on tiptoes to kiss his cheek before pulling away. "I've missed you. And you have perfect timing. My shift just ended."

He swallowed the sudden lump in his throat and smiled down at her. "I've missed you, too. Although Atlanta seems to be agreeing with you."

"It really does," she said, blushing a little.

"I can tell." She barely looked like the same woman he'd banished from Africa all those months ago. The sparkle was back in her silver eyes, the shine back in her short, blonde hair. Her skin glowed and her smile was wide and unfettered. Her time here in Atlanta—and with Simon—had obviously been good for her.

He ignored the lingering pain that awareness caused, focusing instead on the sweet realization that Amanda really was okay. That was enough, more than enough, to make up for any hurt he might be feeling.

"I'm so glad you came," she told him, giving him another quick hug. "I've been waiting for you to get here forever."

"I'm sorry I'm late. I got…" His voice trailed off, his excuses drying up as surely as the deserts of North Africa. He never had been able to lie worth a damn, especially not to Amanda.

"No excuses," she told him, reaching for his hand. "You're here now. That's what's important."

He watched as she examined the still raw scars on his hand. Scars where the bullet went in. Scars from where the doctors at the American University of Cairo had struggled to save his hand. Even more scars from the three operations in Boston to repair as much of the tendon damage as possible. Two top surgeons had collaborated on his case—one a friend of his father's and one a friend of his—but even their expertise hadn't been enough to help him regain full mobility.

In time, with intensive physical therapy, he'd once again be able to use his right hand to open bottle caps or button small buttons or to do most of the little day-to-day things he'd taken for granted for so much of his life. But no matter how much physical therapy he did, no matter how many exercise reps he forced himself to complete, he would never again hold a scalpel.

Would never again be able to operate.

He could see the knowledge in Amanda's eyes, feel her pity in the soft caress of her fingers over his, and it embarrassed him. Shamed him.

He quickly pulled his hand from her grasp, hating how his inability to perform surgery made him feel like half a man—maybe even less. No wonder he'd never been able to compete with Simon.

"Does it still hurt?" she asked softly, ignoring the No Trespassing signs he'd hastily thrown up. But then, a decade and a half of friendship gave her that privilege. Especially since the last time they'd seen each other had ended up with him drugging her so that Simon could get her out of Africa and back to America where she could get the rest she needed. Next to that, a few questions seemed well within the boundaries of friendship.

"Not really," he prevaricated as he curled the hand in question into a fist.

"Liar." He didn't respond and Amanda sighed, linking her right arm with his left one. "But I won't tell. To everyone else you can be the same old indestructible Jack."

Indestructible. He liked the sound of that. If only it were true.

"So, show me this clinic of yours," he told her, not even trying to hide his desperation to change the subject. "I've been looking forward to seeing what you've been up to."

After giving him another long look—one that told him she still knew him better than anyone else on earth—Amanda led him to the back of the clinic. And into another layer of hell.

CHAPTER TWO

IT HAD BEEN two months since he'd been in a medical establishment as anything but a patient.

Two months since anyone had called him doctor and meant it.

Two months since he'd felt anything but useless.

He knew Amanda had brought him here so that he could see there was life after surgery, life after Africa, but it wasn't working. As she took him by the exam rooms, introduced him to the clinic staff, stopped and talked to a few patients she obviously knew, he only felt worse. On one hand, everything had changed. On the other, nothing had and he was stuck in the middle trying to find a spot for himself when the only place where he wanted to be, was no longer an option for him.

"So, what do you think?" Amanda asked as they wound up the tour in the hallway outside the exam rooms.

"It's great," he told her, meaning it. The clinic, while not wasting money for cosmetic changes, had top of the line equipment and a staff that appeared very well-trained. "You look like you've finally found your place."

"I have." This time, when she smiled, contentment radiated from her. "We do good work here."

"I wouldn't expect anything less."

Amanda was a hell of a doctor and she wouldn't get involved in any establishment that wasn't top-notch. At the thought, For the Children, the organization that funded his clinic in Somali, flashed into his mind. They were a fantastic organization to work for and after two months away, he missed them. Missed practicing medicine. At the same time, though, returning to Africa, where he'd been shot, made him uneasy. Oh, he would never admit it to anyone, but he was beginning to think that his time in Africa was as finished as Amanda's was. The idea filled him with sadness, with more knowledge of how useless he had become.

He shook the uneasiness off, refused to give in to it. So what if he was aimless, directionless, for the first time in his life. Parading his insecurities in front of Amanda was the last thing he wanted to do.

"So, can I buy you a late lunch?" he asked her, glancing at his watch. "I want to take you and Simon to dinner tonight, as well."

"Actually, we were hoping to have you over to the house tonight. Simon's cooking."

Of course he was, as Amanda could scorch water. His stomach tightened a little at the idea of seeing the two of them ensconced together in domestic bliss, but it wasn't like he hadn't known it was coming. He was the one who had emailed Simon, after all. Who had brought him back into Amanda's life.

Which was a good thing, he told himself viciously. The other man had saved her, brought her back to herself after the devastating death of their daughter. Seeing her with him again after all these years was fine. Better than fine, when it meant she was whole and happy and healthy.

"Sure. That'd be great." He added an extra-large grin, so she'd know he meant it.

"Fantastic. And I wish you'd reconsider staying with us." She shot him a reproving look. "We have plenty of room."

Yeah, well, that was where he drew the line. Coming here, making sure she was okay, was one thing. Torturing himself with the knowledge that the woman he'd loved for a decade was down the hall in bed with another man? Call him crazy, but he wasn't that big of a masochist.

"I'm great at the hotel. Honest. Besides, I have to leave for the airport really early in the morning. I don't want to disturb you."

"Airport?" she asked in dismay. "You just got to town last night."

"I know, but I can't stay. I have a physical-therapy appointment in Boston on Thursday. I can't miss it."

"We have physical therapists here in Atlanta, you know."

He ignored the cute little pout her mouth had

worked itself into. "Yes, but I don't live in Atlanta. My doctors are in Boston."

"Boston, Shmoston. You're not happy there. I know you're not."

He sighed, ran a hand through his hair. Resisted the urge to tell her that he didn't have it in him to be happy anywhere. But then he'd sound like the pathetic loser he was, and call him vain, but he wasn't up for any more sympathy.

Not sure what to say, he finally settled on part of the truth. "I'm tired, Amanda. I don't have it in me to try to be someplace new right now. And with the shape my hand is in...I can't be a doctor right now. I can't—"

"Bullshit."

"Excuse me?" He wouldn't have been as shocked if she'd punched him. Amanda had been circling around him for weeks.

"I said, you're spouting bullshit." She grabbed his arm and yanked him into a small supply closet that he assumed—from the desk and diplomas on the wall—was serving double-duty as her office. "You aren't tired. You're scared and you're drowning in self-pity."

"You're one to talk." The words were out before he could stop them. He saw them hit her, saw their impact, and wished he could take them back. Angry as he was, he had no right to take it out on Amanda. Not when she'd already suffered so much.

But she was nodding, eyes clear and shoulders

straight. "Exactly. I am one to talk. Because I was where you are not too long ago." Her voice was harsh and direct now, containing none of the sweetness he'd been hearing from her for weeks. It was almost a relief to have her back to normal—somehow it made him feel more like a functioning member of society.

"You did your tough love thing for me not that long ago. Now it's time for me to return the favor."

"It's not the same thing. I'm going to be fine. I just need…" He didn't know what he needed, besides the full use of his hand back. Without that, he had nothing.

"You need a change of scenery."

"I've already got that. Boston is a far cry from Somalia."

"You've never been able to breathe in Boston. We both know that. Your dad has probably already got you signed up to interview at some prestigious family practice—" She broke off when she saw his face. "Are you kidding me, Jack? You really want to take care of women who spend more on plastic surgery in a year than it would take to run this clinic?"

"You're over-simplifying things."

"And you're making them too complicated. Come to Atlanta for a few months, hang out with Simon and me. Do your physical therapy here, and then, when you're ready, when you're healed, you can make a better decision."

"I can do all that in Boston." Admittedly, Amanda wasn't in Boston, but that wasn't exactly a deterrent. He totally accepted that she was married to Simon—was happy, in fact, that things had worked out so well for her. That didn't mean he was dying to spend every day with what he couldn't have right in front of him.

"Yeah, but here you won't have your family making you nuts all the time."

"No, I'll have you poking and prodding at me."

"Someone needs to—"

"Doctor Jacobs!" The shout sounded from the hallway outside Amanda's closed door and was followed quickly by the slap of footsteps against the linoleum floor.

Jack threw open the door to see the triage nurse from the waiting room. "Dr. Zilker said to get you," she said breathlessly. "There's been a shooting. It's bad."

"Which room?" demanded Amanda, already running to the front of the clinic.

"We've got him in exam-room one."

Jack followed her, adrenaline pumping through his system despite himself. "Who's Zilker?"

"One of our residents. He's good, but he's still new—" She broke off as they entered the exam room and Jack knew why. There was blood everywhere.

For a second, he flashed back to that operating room in Somalia. The one where he'd lost both his patient and his ability to perform surgery. His bum leg shook and he was almost certain he was going to land on his ass.

But then Amanda took control, demanding vitals as she slipped on a pair of gloves before diving right into the mess. Somehow the normalcy of being in the middle of an emergency with Amanda steadied him, had him striding forward and pulling on a pair of gloves, as well. He struggled a little with the right one, but refused to let it back him off.

"What have we got?" he demanded of the resident, who was standing at the front of the bed, his face as white as the sheets on the bed.

His voice must have carried enough authority to make up for the fact that he was a stranger because Zilker didn't hesitate as he stuttered out, "Male, age eighteen to twenty. Multiple gunshot wounds to the chest, pelvis, upper thigh. Blood pressure is seventy over forty and falling…"

The world narrowed the way it always did for him in situations like these. "Do you have blood?" he asked Amanda.

"Yeah. Type him. And call 911," Amanda said, as she went for the wound in the kid's pelvis.

Which left the chest wound to him. It shouldn't come as such a surprise—after all, that was how they always worked, but it did. He looked at the gaping hole in the kid's chest, and wished for his old dexterity. For his ability to get in there and stitch things up.

So great was the longing that he almost walked away, had actually taken a step back when Amanda looked up and pinned him with silver eyes made steely with determination. "Do you think he cares about your hand, Jack?" she snapped at him. "Get in there, get the bleeding stopped enough that the ambulance can transport him to County for surgery or he's going to die. I've got a mess down here. If I try to leave it, he's going to bleed out."

Her words, and the absolute lack of doubt she conveyed, snapped him out of it. Had him moving forward despite his fear and anger, barking out orders to the resident and two nurses standing next to him.

The next twenty minutes passed in a blur of concentration and pain as he forced his stiff hand into positions it hadn't attempted in two very long months. Amanda worked beside him, dealing with the wounds on the kid's lower body as he struggled to stop the bleeding in his chest long enough for the paramedics to be able to take over.

In the old days, he would have said to hell with it and started stitching the boy up, but he didn't have the small motor skills necessary to do that anymore. So he concentrated on basic emergency triage, doing what any other family practitioner or internist would do in the same situation. It wasn't clean, and it wasn't pretty, but eventually the patient was stable enough to be rushed to the nearest O.R.

Before he knew it, paramedics were at the door. Stepping back, he gestured for them to take over. He and Amanda had done all they could.

Stripping off his gloves, he looked down at himself. He was covered in blood, as neither he nor Amanda had taken time to gown up. Which was fine for her, as she probably kept a spare set of clothes around here somewhere, but he looked like he'd just gotten out of a war zone. Not the best look for someone who had to walk through a hotel lobby before getting to his room to clean up.

"We have a few pairs of scrubs in the back that will probably fit you," Amanda told him, having read his mind. "You and Lucas are about the same size."

"Lucas?" he asked.

"My boss. Our boss, if you decide to take the job. This clinic is his baby."

"Oh. Right." This wasn't Amanda's clinic. Wouldn't be his clinic if he decided to take a chance on Atlanta, to take a chance on this job. Which was one more strike against the idea, in his opinion. He hadn't had to answer to anyone in a long time. After running clinics in some of the most remote places on earth for almost his entire career, the idea that he would have to step back and let someone else be in charge, grated. Big time. If he was being honest, he wasn't sure he could work that way.

He didn't give voice to any of his doubts, but then he didn't have to. He and Amanda had known each other a long time.

"You'll be fine," she told him. "Lucas is great to work for. Even a big, bad surgeon like yourself won't have any complaints."

He wasn't so sure. But instead of trying to explain himself, he simply said, "I'm not a surgeon anymore. I couldn't even sew that kid up." He jerked his chin toward their unconscious patient, who the paramedics were prepping for travel.

Amanda didn't flinch, didn't make excuses. Met his eyes straight on and said, "So what?"

He goggled at her. "Excuse me?"

"So you couldn't sew him up. So you can't do everything. So you're not as damn perfect as you want to be. So what? You're still a damn good doctor, one of the best I've ever seen." Her voice was strong, firm, passionate. And pitched low enough that no one else in the room could hear what she was saying. "You saved that kid's life."

"He's not safe yet. There's a lot more work to be done on him."

She made a sound of frustration in the back of her throat. "You know what I mean."

"I know that if I could still use my hand properly, that kid would have a much better chance of survival than he currently does."

"Yeah, and if you hadn't been here, he would already be dead. I'm a damn good doctor, but I couldn't have dealt with the chest and pelvis at the same time. So take what you can from that and move on. You did your best."

"What if my best isn't good enough?" he asked, hating that he sounded like a whiny little boy, but unable to stop the words from tumbling out.

Amanda sighed, then grabbed his arm and yanked him out of the room. For a long time, they didn't say anything. They squared off in the hallway in a stare down of epic proportions.

Amanda blinked first. "What if it is good enough?" she asked. "You've got a gift, Jack. Surgeon or not, you can do things, see things, that no one else can."

"There are a lot of great doctors out there, Amanda." He gestured to her. "And in here. We know that kid would have been better off with a surgeon who had full use of his hands, too. We can debate this all day. In fact, why don't—"

Amanda held up a hand, stopping him mid-breath. "Is working here the same as doing surgery in some fancy Boston hospital? No, of course not. But it's still good work. Still necessary work. You never wanted that life, anyway. Driving a silver Ferrari and doing weekends on Martha's Vineyard. That's no more you, than it is me."

"No, that wasn't where I was headed in my life and it wasn't what I miss. I was happy in Africa, doing surgery for For the Children. Was it frustrating? Yes. Were there times I wanted to quit? Absolutely. But it was good work. Important work. You're damn right I miss it."

"And as soon as you heal, you can go back. I know you want to, even though the rest of us would rather you didn't. The fact of the matter is, you could so easily have died in that clinic in Somalia, Jack. You—"

"I know that."

"Do you, really? Because I think you and your God complex have somehow managed to forget it.

Another man, a weaker man, would have given in to the pain and the blood loss and those bastards who wanted you dead. But you didn't. You're still here. Are you hurt? Absolutely. Has your life taken a twist you weren't ready for? No doubt. Welcome to the world of being human, Jack. That's what happens. It's messy and it hurts and rarely goes according to plan. But that's okay, because it means you're still alive. And you are, Jack, whether you wish you'd given up back there or not. So isn't it time you started acting like it?"

He didn't answer her. He was afraid that if he did he'd lash out at her with words no one needed to hear, let alone Amanda. It wasn't that long ago that she'd been an emotional wreck, a couple short steps from working herself to death because she couldn't deal with the loss of her only child.

He'd been the one lecturing her then and the fact that things had changed so completely made him feel worse. In the space of two months, his whole world had turned upside down and he didn't know what to do about it. Every time he tried to imagine his future without surgery, every time he tried to picture himself in six months or a year or five years, he drew nothing but a blank. If he wasn't a surgeon, if he wasn't a doctor for For the Children, then what the hell was he?

The answer came back to him the same as it always did these days. He was nothing. Working at some low-income clinic in Atlanta wasn't going to change all that.

Panic overwhelmed him and he started to tremble. He was on the verge of shaking apart, the emotional pain of his loss combining with the pain in his hand and leg, spreading through his whole body until he couldn't think. Couldn't breathe. The specter of everything he'd lost rose up inside him, paralyzing him.

On top of that, he was afraid he couldn't hide it, especially from someone who knew him as well as Amanda. If she noticed, however, it didn't matter, because she wasn't letting up. "We need you, Jack." She stepped forward and put one soft hand on his forearm. "We really need you." What she didn't say, but what hung in the air between them, was the fact that he needed this clinic, needed her, at least as much as it needed him.

Sensing his weakness, she pressed her advantage. "Come on, give us a month. What's the worst that can happen?"

His heart was beating too fast and he swore he felt a panic attack coming on for the first time in his life. He tamped down on it even as her question circled around and around in his head. What was the worst that could happen? How about complete and total humiliation? Or him losing even more faith in himself and his skills?

Or, God forbid, him killing someone who could

have been saved because his damn hand wouldn't work right?

The possibilities were endless and he started to tell Amanda so, to list the number of really terrible things that could happen. But one look at her face told him she wouldn't listen. Her mind was made up. Besides, it wasn't like he wanted to shout out his deepest insecurities for the world—or his best friend—to hear. That had never been his style.

Instead, he looked down at his bloodstained clothes and thought of the boy they had saved. Then glanced back into the room at the ripped-up clothes and blood-soaked gauze, and at the patient who was even now being strapped to a gurney to be transported to the hospital.

Yes, he was afraid—desperately afraid—of not being able to do what needed to be done here. But he was even more afraid that if he went back home to Boston he'd end up selling out. Giving in. Becoming the kind of doctor his parents had always wanted him to be—the kind he'd always despised.

And then he knew. Even with everything that could go wrong, with all the mistakes he could make, he would still rather be here, doing something truly helpful, than sitting at home, selling out and feeling sorry for himself.

A sense of relief washed over him. His heartbeat slowed and he could breathe again. Panic subsided into a calm clarity. Working at this clinic with Amanda wouldn't be forever—he couldn't afford to let it be—but for now it was a million times better than the alternative.

He wadded up the gloves he was still holding and—using his good hand—lobbed them at the trash can. They soared into the center of the basket in a perfect three pointer.

Then he turned to Amanda with the closest thing to a smile he could manage. "You're right. It's better than Boston. Looks like you've got yourself a doctor."

CHAPTER THREE

CLIMBING THE FRONT steps that led to the small house he'd rented in the same upper-middle class area of Atlanta that Amanda lived in, Jack couldn't believe how tired he was. In Africa, he regularly worked sixteen or eighteen hour days in an effort to keep up with the never-ending patient load, while today he'd only put in half a shift—five hours—yet he was completely exhausted.

Admittedly, it was his first day on the job. And it had come after a ten-day whirlwind in which he'd packed up his necessities in Boston, moved them all to Atlanta, found a place to rent, visited various medical specialists Lucas had recommended, and started an intense, three-day-a-week course of physical therapy.

But still, he'd figured he was in better shape than this. How had two and a half months off the job turned him into such a wimp? He ignored the voice in his head that told him his weakness had a lot more to do with two bullets and three surgeries than it did the time he'd been forced to take off work.

He loosened his tie and headed into the kitchen

for a glass of iced tea. Grimacing as he took a sip of the too-sweet liquid, he tried to appreciate the drink that was a hallmark of his newly adopted city. It was difficult, though, especially considering he much preferred a cold beer at the end of a long day. But, ostensibly, he was still on pain medication. The little white pills he'd been prescribed did not react well with alcohol.

Not that he was actually taking them regularly anymore. Though his doctor, his physical therapist and his own medical training all told him that he needed to keep a steady supply of the anti-inflammatory and pain medication in his bloodstream if he expected it to do its job, he couldn't force himself to keep up with them anymore. It was stupid, he knew, but he hated the crutch. Hated the need to depend on something else—even a pill—to make himself feel better. He'd gotten through his entire adult life without having to rely on anyone or anything and damn it, he would get through this, too. Even if it killed him.

Which it wouldn't, he assured himself as he took another long swallow of the sweet tea. After all, he didn't completely ignore his doctor' orders. He took the pills when he really needed them—mainly on nights when insomnia struck, because if there was one thing he hated more than depending on the medication, it was lying in bed and staring at the still unfamiliar ceiling, wondering how in the hell he had gotten himself here, to this point.

Opening the fridge, he tried to drum up some enthusiasm as he stared at the fresh produce filling nearly all the available shelves. Amanda had come over the other day, loaded down with bags from her garden and the local farmer's market, and stocked him up. Which he appreciated. He really did. He hadn't been very hungry lately.

Grabbing an apple, he made his way slowly through the house to the back porch. It was what had sold him on the place to begin with. Most of the house was pretty non-descript—typical rental property—except for the backyard. There was a huge porch that ran the length of the house and looked out over a garden that would fit better at a country estate than a small, city property.

Lush plants and flowers took up nearly every square inch, their eminent domain broken only by small walking paths that twisted and turned throughout the backyard. He'd explored them all his first couple of days in the house, had found a rose garden with a bench and the remnants of a vegetable garden. Maybe, if his hand came back enough, he'd start his own vegetable garden this spring.

If he was still here, that was. He might be long gone by then. Back to Boston, maybe. Or more likely, back to Somalia. Or some other war-torn country that was in such desperate need of doctors that they didn't mind broken ones.

Uneasiness twisted in his stomach at the idea of going back to For the Children, back to another war zone where anything could happen. But Jack ignored it and settled himself on the big, comfy swing. He didn't need to think about that now, or about anything, really. He could just sit here and relax for a while. Eat his apple and contemplate nothing more difficult than what vegetables he would plant if he was still around in a few months. Maybe some carrots. Tomatoes. He liked red peppers—

A steady stream of water came out of nowhere, hitting him square in the face before dropping a foot to scatter across his blue T-shirt, as well. It stopped for a moment, than a second stream hit him, followed so closely by a third and fourth that he was soaked before he had time to react. Jumping to his feet, he glanced around, trying to figure out where the attack was coming from. Had his sprinkler system gone insane? Was he sitting directly under a rain gutter?

He investigated the roof of the porch, then the empty blue sky above, then looked carefully around his yard.

But there was nothing, no one.

Dropping his apple core on the table next to the swing, he started to jump off the porch but then remembered his bum leg. More annoyed by that than by the fact that he was soaked, he took the steps two at a time instead. Then headed in the direction the water had come from.

He heard them before he saw them, two young voices laughing and whispering and hushing each other even as they rustled the hedge that separated his yard from his next-door neighbor's. "Hey!" he called, making a beeline for the bushes. "Can I help you?"

At that moment, two towheaded little boys peeked their heads out of the foliage, their expressions steely and determined. It was a look reinforced by the huge water guns in their hands, though the bright colors of the guns tempered the effect. "We don't need help from the enemy," one told him in a tough guy voice that matched his soldier act.

"Yeah," said the other, who was clearly younger by a few years, "We're special forces and we've come to bring you in." As he spoke, the first one leveled his water gun straight at Jack's chest.

"The way I see it," the boy continued. "We can do this two ways."

"Oh, yeah?" Jack cocked an eyebrow, and decided what the hell. He could play along. Better than sitting around whining to himself about his pathetic excuse for a life. "And which two ways are those?" he asked in his own tough-guy voice. He even added a little sneer, to keep things interesting.

The boys' eyes grew round with delight and they exchanged a quick look of triumph. But it only took the older one a second to regain his composure and add a snarl of his own to the mix. "Easy. My way or the highway."

"Our way," the younger one corrected him.

"Right. Our way."

Jack grinned. He couldn't help himself. They were

adorable. Plus, it was nice to see two healthy, happy, well-nourished kids. So much better than the children he was used to interacting with. And these two were loaded with confidence, especially the older one. Jack liked it.

"You think this is funny, Punk?" the oldest one demanded, obviously taking his role seriously.

"No. Not at all." Jack forced the smile from his face—and his voice. "I do have a question, though."

His two assailants looked at each other, wide-eyed. Obviously, their plan hadn't included the hostage engaging them in conversation.

It took a minute, but the younger one finally spoke. "Spit it out, scumbag. It can be your last request."

"Well," he said slowly, as if considering his options, even as he geared up for the fight of his life. "Can I have a few minutes? I'd like to say goodbye." He pulled out his cell phone. "It won't take long."

"Geez, mister." The older one looked disgusted as he stepped closer, gesturing emphatically with his gun. "What kind of hostage situation do you think this is? Get moving!"

"The kind where the hostage doesn't go willingly." Jack spun on his good leg, made a mad dash for cover at the closest tree. Then made a beeline for the water tap at the side of the house, regretting bitterly the fact that he hadn't gotten around to buying a hose yet. But at least there was a bucket beneath it.

Using the house for cover, he twisted the tap with

his good hand and waited impatiently for the bucket to fill up. When the two little dictators whipped around the corner, he was going to have a surprise waiting for them. One that, hopefully, got them as wet as they had gotten him.

HER SONS' SHRIEKS split the air as Sophie Connors yanked the last weed out of the vegetable garden she and the boys had planted a few months before. It was doing nicely, she thought, as she sat back on her heels and surveyed the neat rows of greenery beginning to peek out of the dirt. In a couple more months they'd have a pretty good harvest to show for all the hours of planning and planting, watering and fertilizing, discussing and dreaming, that had already gone into it.

Which meant it was time for her to get a new project to work on. Nothing sprang to mind, but she knew one would come eventually. Maybe she could redecorate the boys' rooms—they'd been obsessed with airplanes for weeks now. Or she could try those cooking classes she kept thinking about. This could totally be the year she branched out and learned how to make more than five dishes with any kind of confidence.

More little boy shrieks sounded behind her, and she rose unhurriedly to her feet. Better to let Noah and Kyle get the energy out now, before dinner and bath time, than end up chasing two naked and slippery little boys around the house right as they should be getting ready for bed.

But then the shrieks were followed by war whoops, and not all of them were in her sons' young voices. In fact, a few of the whoops sounded distinctly masculine—deep and rumbly. Since they were followed by a bunch of laughter—and loud cries of "no surrender" from her sons, she figured she'd better go investigate. Hopefully her children hadn't made enemies of the new neighbor quite yet. Usually it took them a week or two.

Although, judging from the sound of it, this one had a pretty decent sense of humor. Which would be a nice change of pace from the last tenant. He had had nothing but contempt for Sophie's boys and though she'd done her best to keep them away from him, she hadn't always succeeded. She tried to keep them in the backyard most of the time, but every once in a while they'd burst into the front. Inevitably, their escape to the front yard had always coincided with Reece's trip to get his newspaper or take out the trash or go for his daily jog.

More shrieks sounded, these ones louder and more high-pitched than the ones that had come before. Sophie broke into a run.

By the time she got to the high hedge that separated her yard from her neighbor's, the boys shrieks had turned to giggles. It soothed the panic that had raced through her at the sound of their distress, but still, she wasn't going to be happy until she saw them.

Scooting through the hedge, she ignored the way the branches ripped at her old gardening T-shirt and scanned her neighbor's yard for her sons. She didn't see them at first and her fear roared back, but then they came flying around the house, their water guns held in clear attack mode, even as they retreated.

Amused, she watched as they dove behind a huge tree. They were small and skinny enough that she could only see their bright red-and-blue weapons. Water guns that were supposed to be in the pool bag and not in use in her neighbor's yard.

Seconds later, the new neighbor came around the corner of the house after them. He wasn't moving as fast as they were, but he was still booking it. In his hands was a large bucket, obviously filled with water. And it looked like he wasn't afraid to use it.

Perhaps Noah and Kyle had finally met their match.

And what a beautiful match he was. The wet, clinging material of his blue T-shirt revealed a heavily muscled chest. His dark hair was shaggy in that way that only a really expensive hair stylist could manage and his jeans, though ripped at the knees, fit his long, muscular thighs like a second skin. She couldn't see what color his eyes were from this distance, but she was betting they were the same blue as his shirt. And his broad smile was lighting up his entire face.

Deep inside, she responded to that smile. Even as she told her hormones to settle down and behave, that she wanted no part of this man or any other, a strange, unfamiliar heat burned deep in her stomach. Try as she did to ignore it—as she tended to do with most unwelcome things—Sophie couldn't help wondering if a guy who looked like that, and who obviously had a decent sense of humor, was still single.

Before she could tell herself it was none of her business, the battle started up with renewed energy. Spotting her sons across the yard, the man ran toward them and was hit, full face, with double streams of water. Instead of getting angry, he laughed and continued his pursuit. But the bucket in his hands was sloshing and spilling a little bit with each uneven step.

So he was injured, or he had been. Either way, he was limping and she couldn't help wondering how it had happened. Was he a veteran like her husband had been? And like Jeff, had he been injured in the war?

The thought made her guard drop even more, as did the way he handled it when her children leaped out from behind the tree and let him have it, lock, stock and barrel. Instead of getting mad like most people would—even when Noah nailed him in the eye—he just took the soaking. Then, when his opportunity came, he sent the water in the bucket soaring straight at them. Kyle was quicker than his older brother and managed to get out of the soak zone in time, but Noah took the water head on.

She barely suppressed a laugh at Kyle's smirk of satisfaction and Noah's whoop of shock—and glee—as the cold water hit him. He took off running, squishing with every step, and she knew the war was far from done.

Deciding she wanted in on the action, Sophie hurried back to her own house and turned on the hose. Then, stealthily creeping through the hedge, she snuck across the yard straight toward her boys, who were too busy taunting the neighbor to notice.

He must have seen her coming, but gave nothing away, so that when she pressed the valve on the hose nozzle and opened fire on her kids from behind, they were completely shocked.

Shrieks of delight filled the air as they whirled on her, slamming her with stream after stream of water. But they were no match for her mighty hose—or the neighbor's refilled bucket—and soon the sounds of their surrender rang through the yard.

With a laugh, she reached forward and brushed a hand over Kyle's sodden hair before doing the same to Noah.

"We'll get you next time, Mom!"

"I have no doubt. You would have gotten me this time if I hadn't had the aid of our new neighbor." She looked at him, then realized with a jolt that she'd been wrong about the eyes. They weren't blue. They were a rich, dark amber. She liked them, especially how this glint of amusement and mischief could coexist with that shell-shocked survivor look he, and so many veterans, wore.

Definitely a soldier, she thought, as she extended

a hand toward him. "Hi, I'm Sophie Connors. Mother of these two hoodlums-in-training and your next-door neighbor. It's nice to meet you."

He hesitated for a second, then his hand came up to clasp hers. His grip wasn't as firm as she would have expected from such a muscled arm, but when she glanced down and saw scars marring the skin, she understood why.

Injured hand, injured leg. This man had been through the ringer. And judging from the freshness of the scars, it had been a recent deployment and homecoming.

"I'm Jack Alexander," he said in a deep voice that she couldn't help liking the sound of.

"It's nice to meet you, Jack." She placed a hand on both of her son's shoulders. "And these two water warriors are Noah and Kyle. Thank you so much for putting up with their troublemaking."

He grinned, revealing even, white teeth. "They're not troublemakers. A little high-spirited maybe, but they're great fun to be around."

"I think so." She returned his smile. It was impossible not to like a man who so obviously liked her children. "Welcome to the neighborhood. If you need anything, please let me know."

"Thanks." He didn't say anything else.

As the moment stretched, she gestured toward her house. "Time to come in, boys. Dinner should be almost ready." With a little wave, she turned to go. But she'd only made it a few steps, her boys running ahead of her, before she felt compelled to turn back. "You're welcome to come to dinner. Kind of an apology and welcoming, all in one? It's nothing special, but if you're interested, we'd love to have you."

He took a little while to answer, longer than was strictly considered polite. She didn't blame him, though. Her boys took a little getting used to and, now that she'd impulsively issued the invitation, she was aware of how it probably looked. Single mom on the prowl for hot new neighbor. Could she be more of a cliché?

Except she wasn't on the prowl. Not even close. She felt a little sorry for him. A vet, freshly injured and back from war, trying to put his life back together. It couldn't be easy. He deserved a home-cooked meal, one he didn't have to put together himself.

"No strings," she promised, holding her hands up in mock surrender. "I wanted to say thanks for putting up with my wild ones."

He grimaced. "I wasn't worried about strings. I'm not very good company right now, to be honest."

"My usual dinner companions are eight and five. I love them, but they aren't the most stimulating conversationalists in the world."

"So the bar is low, then?"

She laughed, really liking his droll sense of humor. "Very low. Come on. It's lasagna. Nothing fancy."

"Homemade lasagna?" he asked, his ears perking up.

"Is there another kind?"

"What time do you want me there?"

She glanced at her watch. "Forty-five minutes? That will give me a chance to get the boys cleaned up and a salad made. Sound good?"

"Sounds great."

"Okay, then."

Sophie headed back for the hedge, leaning over to wind the hose as she went. And doing her best not to wonder if he was watching her leave. She hoped not. Her bottom was definitely not her best feature.

CHAPTER FOUR

EXACTLY FORTY-FIVE minutes later, Jack stood at Sophie's door, a half gallon of ice cream in one hand and a bunch of regrets in the other. Why had he said yes? He really wasn't up for socializing, no matter how casual it was. He was exhausted, in pain, and more than a little cranky—though he hated admitting that, as it made him feel like an overwrought toddler. And with a full day at the clinic ahead of him tomorrow, plus another damn physical-therapy appointment, he'd be better off going to bed early. Right now his job and recovery were taking all his energy. He didn't need any more complications. This was the last thing he should be doing right now.

Yet, here he was. About to start a friendship he wasn't the least bit certain he could keep up. He'd rung the doorbell twice, had waited more than long enough to be polite. If he wanted, he could take the melting container of ice cream and head home. After all, he'd lived up to his side of the bargain. He'd shown up, prepared to sit on a hard wooden chair and make uncomfortable small talk when all he really wanted was to be at home nursing his aching leg—the pain exacerbated by the water war.

He tried to tell himself he'd been seduced by the promise of homemade lasagna, but that wasn't strictly true. After all, with his appetite the way it was, he probably wouldn't be able to do the meal justice. Really, any company was better than his own. Pasting on a smile he was far from feeling, he knocked one more time to be thorough, and when there was no answer he was about to turn around and say to hell with it. But then the door flew open. This time, Sophie was the wet one, her bright purple tank top clinging to her in all the right places.

He might not be interested—in dating or in a relationship—but he'd have to be dead not to notice all those lush curves, especially when they were showcased so spectacularly. She had large, full breasts, a tiny waist and hips that his fingers itched to sink into. Her red-gold hair was piled in a messy bun and her green eyes had the same innate amusement he'd seen earlier in the yard. It was a good look on her.

"I'm sorry," she said a little breathlessly, stepping back to let him into her home. "The boys were taking their bath and…" She trailed off with a laugh. "Let's just say they got a little over-enthusiastic. Which, I'm sure you have no trouble imagining."

"They were incredibly subdued when I saw them earlier," he replied, tongue firmly in cheek. He stepped into the foyer.

"I noticed that." She glanced down. "You brought ice cream?"

"I haven't had a chance to pick up any wine. And I figured the boys would appreciate this more, anyway."

"Chocolate-chip cookie dough is a particular favorite around here. You've already passed the cool test with your willingness to join the water fight this afternoon, but this will send you soaring through the stratosphere."

"Thanks, I guess." He didn't know what else to say. He was a little wary of the way she spoke as if her kids had plans to keep him around for a while. He might be the new neighbor, but he had no intention of becoming part of the regular landscape around here. What was the point when he had less than no desire to stick around Atlanta at all?

Even more ill at ease than he'd been previously, Jack followed Sophie through a brightly colored living room filled with children's toys into a friendly, well-lit kitchen. It was nice, not as fancy as the one at his house, but clearly used more often. The walls were a warm yellow and the counters were a dark gray granite. He liked it, especially the bay window above the sink. It was filled with colorful pots holding abundant herbs that filled the room with a rich earthy scent. It reminded him of the time he'd spent in South America.

"Is there anything I can do to help?" he asked to be polite, though he prayed she'd say no. He wanted to help, but his hand hurt from overuse and the muscles were spasming and aching so much that he figured it'd be a miracle if he could hold a fork correctly. He figured it was payback for the three physical-therapy appointments he'd missed during the course of the move.

"Actually, you could put the salad on the table," she told him, nodding to a large wooden bowl on the counter. "I tossed it with olive oil and vinegar before it registered that you might have preferred something else." She flushed a little. "Sorry. We don't get a lot of company, to be honest."

"Oil and vinegar is fine." He used his good hand to lift the bowl and carry it to the wide table at the end of the room. "Everything smells delicious."

"Yeah, well, lasagna's hard to screw up."

He laughed, despite the pain shooting up one arm and down his leg. "You sound surprised."

"No. Relieved," she said with her own laugh. It was a larger than life sound, one that filled the room to the brim with joy. He liked it, too. "Sometimes my cooking can be a little sketchy," she told him. "I have a tendency to get distracted in the middle of a recipe and sometimes things take a turn for the... well, let's call the result *interesting.*"

He must have looked a little alarmed because she hastened to add, "But not with Italian food. I can make spaghetti, fettuccini and lasagna with the best of them. A leftover from my days at Mama Maria's."

"You learned to cook in an Italian restaurant?"

"I learned to cook in an Italian foster home." As soon as the words escaped her mouth, her eyes widened. Like she couldn't believe what she'd told him.

He didn't want to make her feel more uncomfortable by responding. The fact of the matter was, people often told him things they would otherwise keep to themselves. It had been that way for as long as he could remember. For whatever reason, people trusted him and, more often than not, spilled their guts. It never used to bother him, but these days it made him uneasy. Not the confidences, but the trust implicit in them. He didn't deserve that trust, hadn't deserved it since he stood in a Somali clinic and let a bunch of monsters kill his patient and his nurse, both of whom had been under his care. Both of whom he'd been responsible for.

Silence stretched between them, and as guilt rode him hard, he thought about breaking it with a witty comment, a funny anecdote. He had any number of tricks in his slick and charming bag. Or he could say something sincere and comforting, but that might encourage some kind of bonding moment and that was the last thing he wanted. Terrible as it seemed, he didn't have the will or energy for any of this.

Sophie cleared her throat as she fiddled with the necklace that nestled in the hollow of her throat. "Let me get the lasagna on the table and we can eat."

He nodded cautiously. "Sounds good. Thank you."

Before she could say anything else, Kyle came flying into the room, Noah at his heels. "I'm going to kill you!" Sophie's oldest son shouted as he chased his brother around the center island. "Give it back!" he shouted. "It's mine!"

"You lost it. Finders keepers, losers weepers."

"I didn't lose it—you stole it. Now give it to me!"

"Whoa, whoa, whoa," Sophie said, putting a hand on each boys' head to stop them. "What is going on here?"

"Kyle stole Mr. X," Noah whined. "He knew I was looking for it and he took it."

"That's not true. Noah left it in my room yesterday. I was playing with it and when he saw me, he hit me."

"You want me to hit you?" Noah sneered as he lunged at his brother. "That wasn't a hit. That was a love tap."

Sophie slapped a hand on Noah's chest and moved him away a good three paces. Then turned in time to see her youngest making faces behind her back.

Jack could tell it was the last straw. Relaxing in his chair, he waited for the fireworks to begin.

IF THE GROUND opened up and swallowed her now, she'd be totally okay with it. Seriously. An earthquake fracturing a random crack down the middle of her kitchen. It would be better than this. Like it wasn't bad enough that her kids had soaked her wounded neighbor to the skin an hour ago, now they had to start World War Twenty-Seven while he was sitting here watching? Fan-freaking-tastic.

"Give it to me," she said holding her hand out for the action figure. She had to work hard to keep her voice level. After a week of getting up before dawn to work on arguments for the three cases she had going to court in the next couple of weeks, she was running on caffeine and adrenaline and not much else.

"But, Mom," Kyle whined. "He left it in my room. That makes it mine."

"No! I left it there because you distracted me. You couldn't read your stupid baby book so I helped you. Now give it back! It's mine."

"Actually, it's mine!" she told him, wiggling her fingers in a way that the boys knew meant business. Seconds later she was holding the latest cartoon villain and releasing her grip on two sulky little boys. The joys of motherhood were myriad and many, she reminded herself as she herded them to the table. Myriad and many.

Settling herself at the table, she risked a glance at the neighbor. What had possessed her to invite him over for a home-cooked meal? Yes, he'd looked a little lonely and she'd felt bad for him, but now he looked shell-shocked, and she couldn't blame him. In the space of a couple hours, he'd been attacked by water-gun-toting maniacs, blabbered at by her at about a million miles an hour, and now he'd witnessed her children acting like…well, she wasn't going to go there. It was a wonder he hadn't run out screaming into the night.

An awkward silence descended on the table as she dished out the lasagna and garlic bread. Her boys were busy glaring at each other and the neighbor was pursing his lips and looking at everything but her. At first, she thought it was because he was embarrassed or annoyed, but then she realized he was trying to keep from laughing. The knowledge relaxed her immediately, and she dished up the food with a grin instead of a grimace.

"So, Jack," she said after everyone was served. "How are you settling into the house?"

"I'm managing. It's bigger than my last place so I'm going to have to do some shopping to fill it up."

Before she could respond, Noah butted in. "I'm glad you moved in. I like you a lot better than our last neighbor."

Jack turned to him, a bemused look on his face. "You don't know me."

"Yeah, well, old prune face would never have a water fight with us!"

Jack looked at her, baffled, like he had no idea whether to laugh or wait for her to scold the boy. Sophie smiled. She knew she should admonish her son but Reece really had been an old prune face, despite being under thirty. "Tommy brought a frog to school today!" Kyle contributed. "He had it hidden in his backpack but it got loose when he went in to get his snack. It hopped around the room before landing right in the middle of Mrs. Erickson's desk."

"What did Mrs. Erickson do?" Sophie asked.

"She screamed. Then she grabbed the butterfly net from our science kit and chased it around the room. Which was working until Jackson decided he wanted to help. He knocked over the aquarium and Nessy got out."

Nessy was the class pet—a brown and black python that most of the kids in the class adored. There were a few hold-outs however and Sophie burst out laughing as she imagined the chaos that had to have ensued when Kyle's sweet, soft-spoken kindergarten teacher attempted to capture a wily snake and a frog hell-bent on escape.

"How'd she catch them?" Jack asked. Kyle responded with a vivid tale about the combined efforts of the entire kindergarten class. Everyone, even Noah, laughed. The ice had officially melted.

After dinner, Sophie excused the boys to go play their nightly half hour of video games while she cleaned up the kitchen. As she stood to collect the plates, Jack insisted on helping her carry them to the sink. She wanted to protest—from the way he'd carefully avoided using his right hand during dinner, she could tell it was bothering him. But she was afraid her refusal would hurt his pride.

"So, I can tell from your accent that you're not from Atlanta," she said as they worked together.

He cleared his throat. "No, I'm from Boston."

"That's the accent I'm hearing. I knew it wasn't Southern, but I couldn't quite place it. What brings you here?"

"Work. A friend of mine runs a clinic down here and she needed a hand. I wanted a change of scenery, so here I am."

"A clinic? You're a—"

"I'm a trauma surgeon." He choked a little, then corrected himself. "I'm a doctor."

She glanced at his injured hand, which clearly wouldn't be much help in a delicate surgery. It was balled into a fist where it rested against his thigh, the scars a livid purple white against his tanned skin. She had an overwhelming urge to reach out and stroke them, but she withheld the urge. Which was a good thing because when she looked up again, he was scowling at her.

An apology trembled on the tip of her tongue. She was embarrassed to be caught staring and felt bad because it was obviously a new and touchy subject for him. But she found herself unable to say she was sorry. Maybe it was the way he was looking at her, like he was daring her to say something. Or maybe it was the way he was so obviously caught up in the pain and confusion of having to be something different than what he'd always been.

She could relate to that. She'd had to reinvent herself a couple times so far—once when she was eighteen and had finally escaped from the foster-care system and again after Jeff had died in Afghanistan and she'd been left to raise two little boys alone. Neither time had been easy, but she'd made it through just fine.

But it seemed ridiculous to ignore his injury when they were both so aware of it. She'd hated it when she'd run into people after Jeff had died and they'd either drown her in pity or ignore the subject like it had never happened, even though it was written all over their faces So she decided to simply be straightforward about his injury.

"What happened?" she asked. "If you don't mind me asking, I mean."

His face turned a mottled red and when he answered he was looking at a spot over her shoulder instead of directly at her face. "I was shot."

Her knees shook a little, before she locked them in place. Jeff had died from gunshot wounds. "In Iraq?"

"No." He looked at her strangely. "Why would you think that?"

"I'm sorry. With your injuries, I figured you were a veteran—"

"I already told you. I'm a doctor."

"I know. It's just…not many civilian doctors get themselves shot."

"I didn't get myself shot." He spoke so softly and precisely that she could tell she'd touched another sore spot.

"I'm sorry. I seem to be putting my foot in it a lot today. I didn't mean that the way it came out. We can talk about something else if it will make you feel better." He'd tensed up so much that she really wished she'd never brought the subject up. Maybe he didn't feel the same way she did, that it was better to get the elephant in the room out in the open rather than hide it behind a sheer curtain three sizes too small. She hoped she hadn't made a terrible mistake.

He didn't answer for a while. She was about to attempt to broach some other, much less harmful subject—although she didn't have a clue what that might be—when he said, "I was operating on a patient when it happened."

"In Boston?" She couldn't imagine a gunman getting into the operating room of a major hospital.

"In Somalia. I ran a clinic for a charity organization there."

"Really? Which one?"

"For the Children. We're a non-profit organization that goes into war-torn and disaster-stricken nations to establish medical care for people who wouldn't otherwise have access to it."

"I know who they are. I contribute every year during their big fundraising drive."

He lifted an eyebrow. "From someone who's worked for more than a decade in clinics that have benefitted from those donations, thank you."

"I really admire what your organization does. It's amazing to me the way you put your whole life on hold to help others."

"My life wasn't on hold. Going to those countries, working with For the Children, that was my life." As soon as the words came out he looked sick, like he wanted nothing more than to never have said them.

Sophie thought she knew what it was like to have your whole life taken away with one pull of the trigger. She'd thought, when Jeff died, that everything had changed. But in the months that followed, she realized that in fact little had changed. Yes, she'd lost her husband. Yes, the boys had lost their father. But the truth was, Jeff had been gone more than he'd been around during their entire married life. Three tours in Iraq and one in Afghanistan had created a life at home, with the boys and with her career, that operated independently of him. And after he died, in a way, it simply continued that way.

Looking at Jack, hearing his story and seeing the small amount of pain he had exposed to her made her see that life had indeed changed irrevocably for Jack. With the injury to his operating hand and the trauma from being shot in the very clinic where he worked, there was probably no chance he could return to the life he loved.

Empathy pierced her and despite her feelings about apologies, she murmured, "I'm really—"

"Don't say it." His tone told her the conversation was closed.

Silence stretched taut between them as she continued to wash dishes and he continued to clear the table. When she could take it no longer, she asked. "So, where's this clinic you're working at now? Is it near here or—"

"It's close to downtown." He set the lasagna pan—the last thing to be brought over from the table—on the stove with an urgency that couldn't be missed. "Thanks for dinner," he continued. "But I should probably get going."

"You don't have to do that."

"It's late and I have work tomorrow." Neither of them commented on the fact that it wasn't yet eight o'clock. He made his way down the hallway, but she stopped him at the front door.

"At least stay for ice cream. I really am sorry. I didn't mean to make you uncomfortable."

"You didn't." It was an obvious lie. "Thank you again for the meal. I guess I'll see you around."

In other words, please don't ever invite me over again. Nice job, Sophie, she told herself as she stepped back, watching as Jack fled. She'd invited him over to welcome him to the neighborhood and had, instead, managed to both hurt and embarrass him. Definitely not one of her better ideas.

Yet as she watched the lights come on in his house, she couldn't help thinking that Jack needed someone to shake him up. Oh, he was doing a good job of coasting along, looking and acting normal. But below the surface lay a seething wound of anger and regret that was festering.

It was none of her business. She knew it wasn't. And yet…and yet she kept seeing him in the yard with her sons. Happy, kind, engaged. A huge grin on his face as he forgot, for a moment, all the pain and rage he had inside.

That's when she knew she wasn't going to be able to leave well enough alone. It looked like she had a new project after all.

CHAPTER FIVE

THE PHONE RANG as Jack was coming in from work. He was tempted to ignore it—only a few people had his house number and he wasn't in the mood to talk to any of them. But he felt that familiar tug of responsibility. What if something was wrong? He answered it.

"Jack?" His mother's smooth, cultured tones slid through the line as soon as he picked it up.

"Hi, Mom."

"How are you feeling?"

"Fine."

"Really?" She sounded hopeful.

No, not really. His leg throbbed and he'd had to pass two patients on to one of the residents today because they needed stitches he couldn't do. "Absolutely."

"Oh, good. I'm so glad to hear that."

Of course she was. It was so much easier to move on with life when one's son wasn't mucking it up by getting shot. "Do you need something, Mom? I just got in and I want to take a shower."

"Your father and I are celebrating our fortieth

wedding anniversary next month and I've decided to throw a party. Naturally, we want you to be there. Especially since you missed the one we threw for our thirty-fifth." Five years had passed and Jack could still hear the note of accusation in her voice.

"I was in Rwanda, Mom. It wasn't like I was around the block and refused to come."

"Of course not. But now that you're so much closer, there should be no excuses." There was a will of steel running through the conciliatory words. "Besides, it will give your dad a chance to check you over, make sure you're healing all right."

"Dad's not an orthopedist, Mom."

"He's a doctor. And we're both worried about you."

Jack sighed. Of all the things he hated about his damn injury, this definitely made the top two. His relationship with his parents, at least up until the shooting, could be described as a benign disagreement. His parents loved him, he loved them. They'd provided him with everything a kid could ever need and in return, he'd graduated top of his high school class, went on to Johns Hopkins undergrad and Harvard Med—where he graduated second in his class. And then he dared to do the unthinkable—he'd taken a job with For the Children against their wishes—a decision they never understood. Even so, they had still enjoyed trotting out tales of their philanthropist son at dinner parties.

Now that he was injured, he was still refusing to

settle down into the expected, and ritzy, path of private practice. But their interest had taken a sharp upswing. Suddenly his mother was calling him regularly to check on him, while his sister was bombarding him with emailed articles about post-traumatic stress disorder and learning to live with disabilities. Even his father was getting in on the act, albeit more subtly. Even though Jack had taken the position at the clinic, and made it clear he had every intention of going back to Africa once his physical therapy was over, he continued to get interview requests and partnership offers from lucrative practices all over Boston. He knew very well that his father was responsible for every single one.

Jack tolerated their interference for the most part, knowing they were trying to be supportive in their own ways. But it was so unlike the comfortable distance that had existed before the shooting—and so much more intrusive than he wanted to deal with right now—that he didn't quite know how to respond. So, with a silent apology to his sister, he very deliberately threw her under the bus.

"How's Anna doing, Mom?" he asked. "Is everything going okay with her pregnancy now?"

His mother gasped. "Why? Was something wrong that I didn't know about?" Her voice rose in alarm, a little higher with each word she spoke.

"I'm sure everything's good now. I was just checking." He smiled as he said it, because he knew everything was perfectly fine with his sister. And he knew he was going to get an irate phone call from her later in the evening, right after their mother got done interrogating her about the baby—the other favorite topic in the Alexander household. It was a crappy thing to do, he was the first to admit it, but Anna would understand. When his mother got like this, it was every Alexander for him or herself.

As they were hanging up—his mother now anxious to get off the phone and assure herself that all was well with her youngest child—Jack wandered over to the window and glanced out at the street in front of his house.

Noah and Kyle were riding their bikes on the sidewalk, going four houses away from their own and then turning around and riding four houses back. He watched them for a minute as he thought about the disastrous dinner he'd had at their house the week before. He wanted to blame it all on Sophie—she had been pretty pushy, after all. But at the same time, he was the one who hadn't handled her questions well. After all, he was the one who had run away rather than deal with the feelings her questions had brought up.

He didn't like explaining what had happened to him, didn't like showing weakness in front of anyone, let alone a woman he barely knew. That was why he'd been so frustrated today at the clinic when he hadn't been able to stitch up those patients. It had been humiliating to have to get help from kids who were barely out of med school, even more humiliating to have them look at him with pity and relief that they weren't in the same situation. Relief that they were whole.

Outside, the boys were calling back and forth to each other, laughing as they tried to do stunts on their bikes. Noah rode off the curb, did three big circles in the street to gain momentum before riding hell bent for leather straight at the sidewalk. At the last minute he pulled up on his handlebars and jumped the curb.

Kyle congratulated him, gave him a high five, and then rode carefully down his driveway into the street. Jack stiffened, glancing toward Sophie's house, expecting her to run down the driveway toward the kindergartener at any second. It was one thing for his eight-year-old brother to do it, but Kyle looked unsteady on the bike, like he'd just learned how to ride a two-wheeler. Letting him jump a curb seemed like a supremely stupid idea.

As Kyle circled like his brother had before him, going faster and faster, Jack knew that was exactly what he was going to attempt. And since Sophie didn't seem to be coming to put a stop to it, Jack rushed toward the door himself. Maybe it was none of his business, but the kid was going to—

He was too late. Unable to complete the jump, Kyle crashed into the curb and went down hard in the middle of the street—at the same time a car sped around the corner. Jack started running, his heart pumping triple time as he cursed his bum leg and the fact that he was nowhere near as fast as he used to be. Noah screamed and dove into the street after his brother and for five of the longest seconds of his life, Jack was terrified they'd both be hit.

The car, blasting loud music and driven by a teenager holding a cell phone, swerved at the last second, honking loudly as it passed the boys. Jack stumbled as relief swept through him.

By the time he reached them, a visibly shaken Noah had helped a crying Kyle out of the street. The poor kid was all torn up—elbows and knees skinned and what looked like the beginning of a black eye from where handlebars had probably hit him in the face.

"Hey, now, you're okay," Jack said, ignoring the burning in his leg to squat down so that he was face to face with Kyle.

"It hurts!" the little boy wailed.

"I know it does. What do you say we go to my house and I'll clean you up."

Noah eyed him suspiciously and he couldn't help grinning. He really liked this kid and the fierceness he brought to every situation. "My mom says we shouldn't go to anybody's house when she's not home."

He lifted an eyebrow in surprise. "Your mom's not home?"

"No. She's still at work."

"What about your babysitter?"

"She didn't meet us at the bus stop today so we walked home alone."

And had been alone ever since, Jack surmised. Three hours was long enough for two little boys to get themselves into trouble.

Kyle, sensing he'd lost both of their attention, started to wail louder. Jack scooped him into a hug and then stood, the boy still in his arms. He turned to Noah.

"While I agree that you shouldn't ever go anywhere your mom doesn't know about, I'm going to make a case for breaking that rule just this once. One, because I live right next door and we can watch for your mom out the window. And two, because I'm a doctor and I'd really like to check and clean out Kyle's scrapes." Not to mention get the boy to calm down long enough for him to get a good look in his eyes. If a shiner was already appearing, the kid must have hit his head pretty hard. He could have a concussion.

Kyle quit screaming and asked, "You're a doctor?"

"I am."

Noah considered carefully before agreeing with Jack. "And if you could do something about his black eye before Mom gets home, that'd be great. 'Cuz she's going to flip when she sees it."

Jack had a feeling Sophie was going to flip about lots of things, but he could understand Noah's concern. He had started the whole curb jumping thing, and he was the oldest, so he was going to be in for it when Sophie got a look at Kyle.

"What time does your mom usually get home?" he asked.

"Five on Monday, Wednesday and Fridays. Six-thirty on Tuesdays and Thursdays."

He glanced at his watch. "That gives us about twenty minutes. I'll do my best to play down the war wounds in that time. Sound good?"

"Sounds great," was Noah's heartfelt answer. Even Kyle nodded along from where he nestled his head against Jack's shoulder.

Jack carried Kyle into his kitchen, where he set up a makeshift infirmary consisting of gauze, peroxide, antibiotic ointment, band-aids, a flashlight and ice. Kyle's eyes widened when he saw the line-up of medical supplies and he forgot to cry in his fascination. "What's the flashlight for?" he asked.

"To look in your eyes."

"What are you looking for?"

"I need to know if the fall shook your brain up a little bit."

"You can see that in my eyes?"

"Cool!" Noah exclaimed. "Kyle's brains are leaking into his eyes!"

"What? *No!*" Kyle squeezed his good eye shut as tightly as he could.

"What are you doing?" Jack asked.

"Keeping my brains from leaking out."

Jack couldn't help it. He laughed.

"It's not funny. I need my brains," Kyle howled. "I don't want them to leak out. Don't let them leak out, Dr. Jack."

"They're not going to, I promise. First of all, one of your eyes is almost completely swollen shut, so nothing is leaking out that one. And if you'll open the second and let me get a good look, I'll prove to you that nothing's leaking there, either."

Kyle slit his good eye open barely, but Jack could nonetheless see the doubt shining from it. "What kind of doctor are you again?"

"The kind who can check for brain leakage."

The eye opened a little more. "Anything there, Doc?"

This time Jack held the laughter that was welling up inside him long enough to say, "Nothing so far. I think we're safe."

"Schwoo," Kyle sighed heavily, wiping one little hand across his forehead. But he dropped it when Jack reached for the flashlight. "I thought you said we were safe."

"On the brain leaking part. But I still need to make sure your brains didn't get spun around like a milkshake in there. So open up for a second."

Kyle did as he was told, and Jack watched as the boy's pupil shrank in reaction to the light. He glanced over at the other eye. He really wanted a look at that pupil too, to ensure both were the same size. But trying to pry it open would hurt Kyle and he really didn't want to do that—the kid was being such a trooper.

"No milkshake?" Kyle asked as he put the flashlight down.

"No milkshake." He held up three fingers. "How many fingers am I holding up?"

"Three!" Noah crowed.

"Good, though I wasn't exactly asking you. This is more milkshake brain stuff."

"Oh. Sorry."

Jack turned back to Kyle, this time only holding up one finger. "How many?"

Kyle gave the right answer and after a couple more questions to rule out the likelihood of a concussion, Jack moved on to the various cuts and scrapes.

"You know," he said, checking the worst of the bunch out first, "There are easier ways to injure yourself than kamikaze biking."

"We were practicing for the X games. We want to be alternative sports heroes."

"Alternative sports, huh?" He was trying to distract the patient from what he was doing, but it didn't work. Kyle cried out as he poured peroxide over the scrapes, and Jack winced a little himself. The kid was really being a trooper and he hated to hurt him, even if it was for his own good.

"Yeah," Noah said, "We want to be snowboarders."

"Good luck with that. I didn't realize Atlanta was known for its prime snowboarding slopes." He squeezed some ointment onto the wound before moving on to the next.

Kyle sighed. "That's what Mom says. But she promised she'd get us skateboards for our birthdays."

"Excellent. Do you know what kind of skateboards you want?"

As the boys babbled out long, convoluted answers that dealt with colors and brand names and wheel types, Jack grabbed tweezers from his medical bag and extracted a few pieces of gravel from Kyle's skinned knee. The boy was so wrapped up in discussing his future skateboard that he didn't even notice, which was exactly what Jack had intended.

The boys kept up a steady stream of chatter for the next ten minutes with very little prompting from him. By the time they'd wound down, they'd covered everything from famous skateboarders to their new video game to who the best superhero villain combo was and Jack had finished cleaning all of Kyle's scrapes.

When he started gathering up the detritus from the great-bicycle-wound operation, however, Kyle's lower lip started to tremble a little. "What's wrong, buddy?"

"My knee hurts."

"I know it does. But the ointment had some special pain killing stuff in it, so give it a few minutes to work. It'll feel much better."

"Mommy always kisses my boo-boos."

"I bet she does." He checked the clock across

the room, which read six-thirty. "She'll probably be home in a few minutes and then she can kiss it better."

Kyle's lip shook even more as tears bloomed in his eyes. "It won't feel better without a kiss!"

It took him a minute, but Jack finally figured out what Kyle was getting at. "You want me to kiss your boo-boo?" He felt a little ridiculous using the word boo-boo, but Kyle nodded vigorously. Which is how Jack found himself leaning down and kissing the band-aid over Kyle's right knee. It was the first time in his life he could ever remember doing such a thing, but surprisingly, it didn't feel nearly as strange as he would have thought.

"Noah, why don't you go look out the window in the living room and watch for your mom while I make us some hot chocolate. I don't want her to come home and find you missing."

"You have hot chocolate?" Kyle said, eyes suddenly wide as saucers. He bounded up from the chair, injuries forgotten. "I love hot chocolate!"

"How about marshmallows? Do you have those?" Noah asked.

"I don't, sorry." The only reason he even had hot chocolate was because it was Amanda's favorite. He'd picked a box up at the store the other day so he'd have it for her the next time she came by—which he knew was stupid and smacked vaguely of emotional suicide, but he hadn't been able to help himself. "Do you want something else?"

Noah's sigh was long. "No, that's okay."

Jack turned to hide his smile. He didn't want the kid to think he was laughing at him. "Go check on your mom, okay? And I promise, next time I'll have marshmallows and whipped cream!"

"Yay!" Noah galloped down the hallway to the front window, rejoicing the entire way.

Jack winked at Kyle, then crossed to the stove where he set water to boil. Before he could even get the hot chocolate out of the pantry, though, Noah came rushing back in. "Mom's home. Mom's home."

"Oh." He was surprised to realize he was vaguely disappointed. He'd been looking forward to spending a little more time with the boys—their boundless energy kept him from brooding. "I guess you should head on home, then."

"Will you come with us?" Noah looked at him pleadingly.

Jack tempered his first thought, which was no way in hell! Sophie Connor might be a very nice woman—and God knew, she was raising two adorable little boys—but that didn't mean he wanted anything to do with her. Not after her weird interrogation the other night. The last thing he needed was more prodding, especially after talking to his mother.

"You go ahead. Try and catch her before she gets to the house."

"Too late. She must have gotten home early because every light in the house is on."

Shit. His plan for Noah to keep watch obviously

hadn't been as good as he'd thought it was. Sophie was probably frantic after coming home to an empty house.

He switched off the stove, then began herding the boys toward the front door. "Come on. We need to let her know where you are."

Jack moved them along as quickly as he could, but the task of getting them from his house to hers wasn't nearly as easy as he'd expected it to be. Every time he thought he had them under control, one of them would get distracted and wander off so that by the time they made it to their porch—which was lit up as brightly as the rest of the house—he felt like he'd run a marathon.

The boys bounded up the stairs and through the front door, laughing and chattering, and Jack figured his chances of slipping away unnoticed were pretty good. At least until he glanced through the door and saw Sophie's tear-stained, panic-stricken face.

SOPHIE'S RELIEF at seeing her boys bounding through the front door, happy and healthy, was so overwhelming that her knees nearly collapsed beneath her. She'd been home for twenty minutes, freaking out because her babysitter and sons were nowhere to be found.

At first she'd thought Grace, the college student who watched them after school, had taken them to the park for some exercise. But then she'd called Grace on her cell phone and found out that the girl had forgotten to call and let her know she wasn't showing up. That was when she lost it. After checking every room in the house, twice, she'd ended up running around the neighborhood like a crazy woman, screaming for her children. When that hadn't worked, she'd started dialing the numbers of everyone she could possibly imagine them going to for help—all to no avail.

But she'd missed someone, she realized, as Dr. Jack Alexander warily climbed the stairs behind her sons. Suddenly conscious of the tears on her cheeks, she dashed her hands across her face. She'd already interrogated him like a crazy person. The last thing she needed was for him to think she was a crybaby, too.

"Hi, Mom," Noah said, and hearing his little voice—so safe and happy—melted any shot she had at maintaining a stiff upper lip. A sob welled up inside of her and she dropped to her knees beside the two of them, pulling them into her arms as she tried to get control of her wildly fragmented emotions.

She buried her face in Kyle's neck, breathing in his little boy scent, and once again reached for control. "I'm sorry," she told them. "I'm so sorry I wasn't here."

"It's okay, Mom." Noah let himself get hugged for a minute before struggling to break her too-tight grip. "It was fun. We had chips and salsa and played games and rode our bikes. That's how Dr. Jack found us, when Kyle fell off his bike."

He ran the last few words together, like he was

hoping she wouldn't notice them if he said them really fast. Pulling back, she looked at Kyle's face for the first time and saw the black eye she had missed as she had pulled them close.

"What happened?" she demanded, listening intently as the whole, jumbled story came piling out of the boys. By the time they were done, she was shaken up all over again. Her baby had been hurt and she hadn't been here. They'd been home alone and she'd been at work, blissfully immersed in her latest case, never thinking of how much danger—or how much trouble—her kids could get into. The thought was a dagger through her heart.

She didn't do this. She simply wasn't a mother who left her boys alone. She worked to support her family and that meant she couldn't always be with her boys when they might need her. But she always made sure they were taken care of, that someone was there for them when she couldn't be. Because she knew what it was like to be alone, with no one to turn to for help when you needed it.

She'd spent most of her life being shipped from foster home to foster home, doing whatever she wanted because most of the people hadn't cared nearly as much about her as they had about the money that came with her. Oh, there'd been exceptions—Mama Maria, who taught her to cook Italian food and Rose, the councilor who had inspired her own interest in the law—but for the most part she'd raised herself. More than once she'd gotten into trouble simply because she'd been unsupervised and in the wrong place at the wrong time. The idea that her boys, even inadvertently, had been in the same position today, shamed her in a way not much else could.

"You're squeezing me too tight, Mommy!" Kyle complained. "And I'm starving! What's for dinner?"

She brushed tears off her cheeks once again. "I was thinking Rosa's," she said, naming their favorite Mexican restaurant. "And then ice cream for dessert?"

"Yay! That's even better than hot chocolate," Noah cheered.

"Hot chocolate?" she asked, a whole new panic invading. "You know you're not supposed to touch the stove unless I'm in the same room with you."

"Dr. Jack was going to make it for us," Kyle said. "To make my boo-boos feel better."

"Oh, well, that was very nice of Dr. Jack." Climbing back to her feet, she told them, "Go wash your hands and faces and we'll head out.

"Don't run," she called down the hall seconds later when the stampede began.

As soon as the boys were otherwise occupied, she turned to Jack. "Thank you for taking care of them," she told him. "I had no idea they were home alone."

His lips turned up in a lazy half smile that made her stomach flutter. "I figured you didn't. I'm sorry I didn't get to them sooner. I was watching them play, at least until they ventured into the street. Then I was worried, so I started outside to get them back on the sidewalk when Kyle fell." He smiled a little. "But, on the bright side, he did do one hell of a wheelie on his way down."

"Wow. That thought is so reassuring to me."

"Sorry. I forget moms have their own standards for what's cool."

"We do. And wheelies that end in black eyes don't even make the bottom of the list."

"He'll be fine. I checked him over. No sign of a concussion or anything like that."

"Thank God. Again, thanks so much for taking care of my kids. I promise, it won't happen again."

"I told you, it was no big deal. They're great kids."

Her heart warmed at his obvious affection for her sons. "They really are, aren't they? I can't believe they handled being home alone so well. But I'm going to have to get a new babysitter. Grace totally flaked, didn't even bother to let me know she wasn't going to be here today. That's just not cool."

Noah picked that moment to come thundering back into the room, Kyle right behind him. "We're ready for 'Taco Tuesday,' Mom! Let's go."

She glanced at Jack. "You're welcome to join us."

"No, I don't think so." He looked vaguely horrified at the suggestion and it amused her, despite the fact that she'd been in tears a few minutes before.

"Aww, come on. It'll be good for you."

"I beg to differ," he told her archly. "Tacos are not exactly known as health food."

She did laugh then. When Jack forgot to brood,

he really was quite charming. She'd forgotten that in the past few days, as every time she'd run into him he'd been wearing the blackest of scowls. "No, but they are comfort food."

"Not if you grew up in Boston."

"*Please,* Dr. Jack," Kyle begged. "You have to come to dinner. What if my brains start to leak out my eyes? Who's going to stop them?"

Sophie had absolutely no idea what her son was talking about, but whatever it was, it must have worked because Jack ended up grinning from ear to ear. "I guess I'm stuck, then." He held his good hand out for Kyle to high five. "Taco Tuesday it is."

CHAPTER SIX

AFTER THEY STUFFED themselves on chicken tacos, tortilla chips and more queso than any two boys should be able to consume in five meals, Kyle and Noah ran off to the restaurant's playscape, leaving Jack and Sophie alone at their table on the patio. As she watched her boys run away, he couldn't help a wary glance at Sophie's face, trying to gauge what kind of mood she was in. It was humiliating to admit that he was a little afraid of a woman who barely hit five foot three, but he was. The last thing he wanted was a rehash of the other night, when she'd tried to get him to talk about his hand. Some things were better left alone.

But Sophie seemed surprisingly mellow, despite the ten-minute lecture she'd delivered to the boys over dinner about how they were supposed to call her if anything like this afternoon ever happened again.

"Thanks again," she said to him as Noah made a running leap for the monkey bars. "I don't know what I would do if anything ever happened to them. They're my everything."

"I understand." For a second he thought of

Amanda, of how she'd fallen apart when her daughter had died of cancer. "Being a parent is a scary thing."

"It's an amazing thing." Sophie's voice was more fierce than he had ever heard it. "Before the boys came, I spent my whole life wandering from place to place with no real focus. But when they were born, everything changed. They became my whole world. Nothing is more important than they are."

"What about their father?" The words came out before he could stop them, before he even knew he was going to ask about the man. He hoped she took the question in the vein he meant it, a simple exchange of information and nothing else, as he wasn't the least bit interested in her romantically. Not in her sparkling sense of humor or her crazy red hair or the insane curves that had drawn the eye of every man in the restaurant at least once since they'd arrived.

Her smile slowly faded. "He died in Afghanistan four years ago. The boys don't remember him. Even Noah, who was four when he died. But he'd been gone so much of Noah's life—a year in Iraq and almost a full tour in Afghanistan before he was shot... It's been just me and the boys almost since the beginning. He never even saw Kyle."

Jack started to apologize, to voice the mindless platitudes that one said in situations like these, but the knowing look in Sophie's eyes had the words freezing on his tongue. He suddenly understood that this was why she'd pushed him the other day, why she hadn't pretended his injuries didn't exist. She had scars, too. They might be on the inside, where the only people who could see them were the ones she told about them, but that didn't make them any less real. Or any less painful.

How many people had treated her with pity since her husband had died?

How many people had made her feel like less because she no longer had a husband to father her children?

No wonder she'd refused to back away from his pain. She, too, knew what it was like to lose a huge portion of her life overnight.

The knowledge that she understood should have made him easier with her, more relaxed. Instead, it freaked him out. Made him feel like everything inside him was on display. He'd worked hard these past few months to keep his pain under wraps. The last thing he needed was some beautiful woman with a savior complex to come along and try to protect him from himself.

"You're doing a good job with them," he told her. "They really are great kids."

Her smile was blinding. "I think so, too." She took a couple more bites of her last taco, then leveled those serious blue eyes of hers straight at him. "So, tell me more about this clinic you're working at. Where is it? What's it like?"

"Why is it I always feel like I'm being interrogated when you talk to me?"

"Sorry." She blushed a little. "It's the effect of being a lawyer, I guess."

"You're a lawyer?"

"You don't have to sound so surprised."

It was his turn to flush. "Sorry. You don't really fit the picture I have in my head of a lawyer."

"There are all kinds of lawyers."

"I know. And I say that as a compliment. I hope you take it like that."

She popped a chip in her mouth. "I'll consider it. If you answer my questions."

He sighed. "The clinic is good. In some ways it's really different from what I used to do and in other ways, it's exactly the same."

"Is that good or bad?"

He laughed uneasily, wished for a second that the boys would come back and interrupt them. "You don't ask the easy questions, do you?"

"Easy questions have easy answers. Where's the fun in that?"

"I have no idea." He paused, trying to gather his thoughts. "Africa is…Africa is challenging on a soul-deep level and it's hard to understand if you aren't in the middle of it. It's a beautiful continent, and for the most part, is filled with truly beautiful people. Kind. Warm. But they have so many strikes against them that so often, when I'm there, it feels like everything I do is triage. You know?

"Like I'm slapping a bandage on a wound that a little care, a little money, could have prevented. And the bandage is too small, the antibiotics nonexistent. Soon, a cut that never should have happened gets infected, turns fatal, and there's nothing I could do about it. Nothing anyone could do.

"Here it's not like that. Even at the clinic, which exists to serve low-income families without insurance, there's hope. There's enough medicine on the shelves, enough doctors and nurses to go around. Enough food to make sure children don't starve to death right in front of you. It's—" He cringed, embarrassed when he realized how much he'd said. And how much he'd revealed. "Sorry. I didn't mean to monopolize the conversation."

She reached for another chip, ignored his apology. "Are you going to go back? To Africa?"

"Absolutely," he told her, deliberately ignoring the sick feeling he got in his stomach simply saying the word. It was normal to feel a little apprehensive about going back to where he was shot, he reminded himself. There was no reason to make a big deal out of it. As soon as he was back in Somalia things would get back to normal.

"When?"

"I haven't decided yet." Hadn't let himself decide yet. "I need a few more months of physical therapy before it's even an option."

She nodded, but he had the distinct feeling that she didn't believe him. Or maybe that was his own emotion rubbing off on her. And blinding him to the truth. "I think it's great, actually, the way you're getting a new start here. New beginnings makes it easier to move past the pain. You can forget who you were before and concentrate on who you are now."

"What if I liked who I was before?" Jack froze as soon as the words crossed his lips. It was bad enough to think them in the privacy of his own head.

"Never mind." He pushed back from the table, crossed the patio to the playscape. He shoved his hands deep in his pockets and stared at the structure—and the children on it—with blind eyes. What was he doing here? he wondered bitterly. What was he trying to prove to himself...and to her?

"I'm sorry." He heard her speak from behind him. Her hand rested on his shoulder. "I have a habit of sticking my foot in it regularly. Another by-product of my profession, I suppose."

He didn't answer right away, just turned her words over in his head. Yes, she'd poked at him but hell, he'd probably deserved it. He'd poked at enough open wounds that this was probably payback.

"I thought we had an unspoken agreement about holding off on apologies," he finally said, forcing a grin he was far from feeling.

"Yeah, well, that only counts if the person apologizing didn't act like a total and complete ass. Which, I did. So, I'm sorry. Feel free to tell me to mind my own business anytime I cross the line."

"Okay. Mind your own business."

"I'm planning on it." She held out a hand for him to shake. "Friends?"

"Friends," he said, pressing his palm against hers and shaking. It wasn't until after Sophie had withdrawn her hand and gone to call the kids that he realized that, for the first time since he'd been shot, he'd touched someone with his wounded hand without worrying about what they were going to say or how they were going to react.

As they walked out of the restaurant, he tucked the knowledge deep inside himself. He didn't know what it meant, didn't know if there was anything for it to mean. But it felt good, nonetheless, and for now that was enough.

A WEEK LATER, Sophie barely resisted the urge to slam her phone down, hard, as frustration welled up inside her. She'd been working at home for the past few afternoons, trying to find an alternate method of daycare for her boys since Grace obviously had to go. But nothing was working out the way it was supposed to.

She'd put an ad up at the local community college—which was where she had found Grace and her predecessors—but so far she hadn't gotten any bites. Which, frankly, she was almost okay with. It's not like any of the three girls she'd hired so far this year had worked out sparklingly well. Admittedly, Grace was the only one who had completely failed to show up without any warning or notice, but Michaela and Simone had each come with their own problems.

She wished she could afford to pay more, either

for a certified child-sitter service or for one of the after-school daycares in the neighborhood. But for the two boys, either choice would run close to fifteen hundred dollars a month and she didn't have that. It was hard enough to scrape together the eight hundred dollars she paid her regular babysitters. She was still paying off student loans from law school, plus the mortgage and the car payment and all the other expenses that went into running a home. The death settlement she'd gotten from the army after Jeff passed away had already been used to pay down her mortgage so that it was more manageable on a single income.

A little voice in the back of her head whispered that she could afford to pay more if she got a job at a real law firm instead of working for a local network of battered women's shelters. If she went over to corporate America and pulled down a solid, six figure income, she could afford to pay any kind of child care she wanted.

But she wouldn't be happy and she wouldn't be making a difference. She could live with the first, if that meant a better life for her children, but it was difficult to accept the second. She didn't want to charge wealthy people thousands of dollars for a few hours of her time. She wanted to work with people who couldn't afford to buy their way around the system, people who needed help but who had all but given up hope on ever receiving it. People like the girl she'd once been. People like her mother, who had died at the hands of her drunk and abusive boyfriend when Sophie was barely three years old.

People like Annabelle, the woman whose case she was supposed to be going to court with tomorrow. Annabelle had spent the past five years of her life being beaten regularly by her bastard of a husband. She'd called the police on him twice, had tried to leave him three times, but since he was a policeman himself, he always found a way to get around the charges she filed.

This last time, when she'd taken their daughter and left him, he'd stalked her for weeks before nearly running her down with his car. He did it at night, on a side street where she was walking on her way home from her waitressing job, and because there were no witnesses—it was her word against his—the cops had once again let him go. The fact that Annabelle was covered with scratches and bruises from where she'd dived into a huge, thorny rose garden to get away from him, meant absolutely nothing. The policemen who took her statement said she could have done it to herself to make her husband look bad.

It had been six long months since they'd requested a court date to divorce the loser, and now that the date was finally here, the last thing Sophie wanted to do was postpone it. Annabelle was already a nervous wreck, so freaked out at the idea of facing her husband that she had literally made herself sick with it.

No, they needed to get this over and done with.

Quickly. Before he had the chance to go for her again and before she got cold feet and chickened out. Which meant Sophie was going to have to figure out what to do with her boys tomorrow, even if it meant springing for a service that charged forty dollars an hour to watch two kids.

She was picking up the phone to do just that—she could eat peanut-butter sandwiches for a couple of weeks to help off-set the cost—when her attention was attracted by the sound of a lawn mower sputtering to life. She glanced out the window and nearly choked when she saw Jack mowing the grass.

He was dressed in worn jeans that cupped his butt very nicely, and also had a couple of strategic tears over both thighs. His T-shirt was sweaty—he must have been outside for a while before starting up the mower—and molded to his powerful chest and back in all the right places.

She closed her eyes for a second, wondering if it was possible for her retinas to actually be on fire. She might not be in the market for a man, but that didn't mean she couldn't appreciate a gorgeous specimen when she saw one. Even if he was supposed to be just a friend and a project.

She was a little surprised that he was home at— she glanced at the clock—three fifteen in the afternoon. Sophie set aside her case file and decided it was time for a break. She'd baked cookies for the boys that morning and had set aside a small plate for Jack, as well. He might be well-muscled, but he was also too skinny. Being shot had taken a lot out of him, obviously, and it was time for him to start getting some of it back.

She gave him a few minutes to finish up the front lawn. Then, carrying the plate of cookies in one hand and a glass of lemonade in the other, she went out to meet him.

"You have time for a break?" she asked, waving the cookies in front of his nose. She'd had a couple herself and while she'd never be Betty Crocker, even she had to admit that they were pretty good.

"You baked?" he asked, eyebrow raised. His surprise showed how well he'd gotten to know her in the past few weeks.

"They came out of a package. All I had to do was pop them in the oven."

"Still, I'm impressed." He grabbed one and bit into it, a smile on his too-handsome face. She felt her knees start to tremble a little at the sight, but reminded herself she wasn't the swooning type. Especially not over a friend who was due to go back to Africa in very short order.

"Not as impressed as I am. A full day of work under your belt and you still have the energy to be out here mowing?"

"Actually, I haven't been to work yet. We're switching schedules around at the clinic, trying to figure out which way is the most efficient, so I'm on nights for the next couple of weeks."

She felt a completely irrational stab of disappointment at the knowledge that she wasn't going to be seeing much of him for a while. "Wow!" she said to disguise what she was actually feeling. "That should be different for you."

He shrugged. "Not really. I worked nights in Africa all the time."

"And days, too, I bet."

"There were a lot of people who needed help."

And Jack was not one to turn someone away when they needed him. It was one of the qualities she considered so admirable about him.

He stowed the lawn mower in the garage, then nodded to his front porch. "You want to sit down for a couple minutes?"

"Just a couple. The boys are playing upstairs. It was peaceful when I ducked out here, but who knows how long that will last."

"About ten more seconds," Jack said.

She laughed. "Probably."

"No, really about ten seconds." He nodded behind her and she turned in time to see Noah barreling out of the house, soft dart gun in one hand and a plastic grenade in the other. Kyle soon emerged and Styrofoam darts were suddenly flying in all directions.

She sighed. "I have no idea what I did to have such bloodthirsty children."

"You gave birth to boys."

"Is that your expert medical opinion?"

"Yes, it is." He gestured for her to sit, and though Sophie knew she should go break up the war before someone got shot in the eye, she decided to give the boys a chance. Maybe they'd pleasantly surprise her.

"So, how goes the great babysitter hunt?" he asked, picking up another cookie.

"Terrible. It wouldn't be so bad if I didn't have court the rest of the week, but I'm in Judge Davies' courtroom and he's notorious for running us until six o'clock every night."

"I could take them," Jack suggested casually. Too casually, in her opinion.

"Take them where?"

"I mean, I can babysit them. With this new shift, I'm not due into work until eight, so as long as you're home by seven, it should be fine."

Sophie laughed. She couldn't help herself. His offer was sweet, but... She gestured to her boys, who were currently running in circles around the big Magnolia tree near the street. Kyle had shot all of his bullets, and Noah had grabbed them all up, stuffing them into his pockets until they bulged. Then he proceeded to open fire on Kyle, making her youngest child scream in rage even as he retreated.

"I don't think so."

He looked insulted. "You're willing to trust a flaky college kid with your children but you won't trust me, a certified M.D., with their safety?"

"I didn't say that. It's just, I think it's an awful lot for you, don't you?"

He shut down right in front of her. "Oh, right.

Don't want to overtax the cripple by siccing a couple of kids on him."

"That's not what I meant and you know it."

"Oh, I think it's exactly what you meant." He shrugged, like it didn't matter though she could see, quite clearly, that it did. "But whatever. I was trying to help."

"What I was trying to say was that with twelve-hour shifts at the clinic and physical therapy three days a week, isn't your plate already full?"

"My plate's fine, thanks. Again, I'm a doctor. I know how much my injuries can handle."

"I wasn't talking about your injuries. I was talking about your energy level. In case you haven't noticed, they're an armful—which is about four times the size of a handful. After a few particularly long days, even I have fantasies of locking them in separate rooms for a couple of hours. And I'm their mother."

"Fine. You know best." He smiled at her in a perfectly pleasant manner, like their conversation had never happened. Which drove her nuts, not to mention made her feel intensely guilty. She hadn't known him long, but she'd figured out the first night she met him that Jack was a master of suppression and disguise. What she saw on his face, or heard in his voice, was only about two percent of what was really going on beneath the surface.

With a sigh of surrender, she asked, "You really think you can handle them?"

"I know I can handle them," he said with a grin,

now that he knew victory was within reach. "I love kids and your boys are cooler than most."

"Fine, we'll give it a shot. But just until I find someone who can take the job on a more permanent basis."

"That's all I was suggesting to begin with."

She snorted her disbelief. "Is two-hundred dollars a week enough? That's what I usually pay—"

"You're not paying me," he said, obviously horrified by the suggestion. But on this she refused to back down.

"Of course I am. You're providing a service and I need to pay you for that service. It's simple capitalism."

"Do I look like I need the money to you? I'm a *doctor.*" He stressed the word like it meant he was a billionaire, but she knew better.

"For a non-profit clinic. You're not going to convince me you're raking in the big bucks."

"Maybe not, but I can guarantee you I don't need your money." The inflection he put on the sentence had her watching him through narrowed eyes.

"What does that mean? What do you need?"

"I'm not sure yet. Maybe a few return favors, when they come up?"

"You know that's not a problem. I'll be happy to help with whatever you need. You don't need to use it as payment for babysitting my kids."

"Why not? You expect to pay me for doing a favor. Why shouldn't I expect to do the same thing?"

He'd gotten her but good. "You think you're so cute, don't you?"

"I'm adorable. Everyone says so."

If by everyone, he meant every woman between the ages of eighteen and fifty-five, then he was right. Since he'd moved in his front door had been a revolving series of casserole dishes from every woman in the neighborhood.

She started to snark about it a little more—at least in her own head—until she remembered that he was currently eating cookies she'd baked for her sons.

"Fine. We'll use the bartering system. What do you want from me first?"

He eyed her thoughtfully and despite herself, Sophie felt her breath catch a little in her chest. Not that there was anything sexual in his gaze. There wasn't. Not at all—Jack wasn't that kind of sleaze. But at the same time, there was a thoroughness that drew out something deep inside of her, something that hadn't been seen in almost five years. She wasn't sure how she felt about the fact that it seemed to be coming back to life now—especially when her project was to bring him back to life.

"Well?" she asked a little defensively as she crossed her arms over her chest. She really didn't like how exposed she suddenly felt.

"Nothing comes to mind off the top of my head," Jack said. "But believe me, you'll be the first to know when something does."

CHAPTER SEVEN

HE WAS WAITING on his front porch when the school bus dropped the kids off at the end of the street. Now that the time had actually arrived for him to be in charge of two little boys, there was a huge part of him that was standing back, asking What. The. Hell? What the hell had he been thinking to volunteer for this job and what the hell did he think he was going to be able to do to amuse these kids for three hours after school every day?

It had seemed a really good idea when he was standing there talking to Sophie, fresh off his first day at home. He'd spent the morning staring at the walls, going stir-crazy and the afternoon fixing everything he could get his hand around. He'd gone outside and started mowing as a last ditch effort to keep himself sane—and from dwelling on the fact that he should be in Africa, working, not in America trying to fill the time with ridiculous reruns of the most warped reality TV shows he'd ever heard of.

But now that he was faced with the reality of being in charge of Kyle and Noah for the afternoon, he was beginning to think that reality TV didn't sound so bad. Which showed how desperate he had become.

"Dr. Jack, Dr. Jack!" Kyle came running up the walkway, hell-bent for leather. "What are we doing today?"

Sophie had left strict instructions. Snack from 3:00 to 3:15. Homework and silent reading from 3:15 to 4:00. And then free time from 4:00 to 6:00, but only one of those hours could be spent in front of the TV. Which sounded a little Stalinish to Jack, but that wasn't a battle he was going to fight. Sophie's kids equaled Sophie's rules.

"I thought we'd have a snack first. Any suggestions?" he asked the boys.

"Pizza!" shouted Noah.

"Ice cream!" added Kyle.

"Hot dogs!"

"Chocolate-chip cookies!"

"Coke!"

"Lemonade!"

"Gummi bears."

It was a regular smorgasbord of bad choices, and he laughed as he scooted the kids into the house. "I was thinking more along the lines of peanut butter and apples?" He had a brand new jar of peanut butter that he'd run out and bought that morning—after being assured by Sophie that the boys had no peanut allergies.

"*Bor-ing!*" declared Noah, flopping down on a

kitchen chair and looking for all the world as if he'd lost his best friend.

"I hate peanut butter," Kyle told Jack, a serious frown on his little face.

"You hate peanut butter? What kind of kid are you?" he demanded with a grin, crouching down so that he was eye level with the boy. "Well, if you don't like my suggestions, why don't you make some suggestions of your own—ones that do not include junk food," he clarified to prevent Kyle from singing out more inappropriate choices.

"I like cheese and crackers," Noah said.

"Me, too," Kyle agreed. "With apples."

"Sounds like a plan." Within five minutes—only a few minutes off schedule—he had the two boys settled at the kitchen table with their snack and boxes of organic chocolate milk. He was feeling pretty proud of himself, thinking he had this babysitting thing nailed—how hard could it be, after all—when disaster struck.

It hadn't occurred to him to put the straw in the chocolate milk for Kyle, and the little boy had a difficult time doing it on his own. Jack was in the middle of reaching for it when Kyle finally managed to punch a hole in the top. But he was holding the box so hard that chocolate milk squirted up the straw... and all over Noah's face.

Noah screeched.

"It was an accident!" Kyle cried. "I'm sorry. It was an accident."

Noah paid absolutely no mind to the apology, and picking up his own milk box squirted the entire thing across the table at Kyle.

Kyle sat there, frozen, chocolate milk dripping from his eyelashes and down his cheeks while Noah smirked at him. Jack ran for a towel, had started to wipe the kid off when Kyle unfroze. And attacked.

With battle cry, he launched himself across the table and straight onto his brother. Fists and feet flew and Noah went from smirking to screaming in a split second.

While Jack agreed that the kid deserved the fists—and the feet, he figured his role as adult baby-sitter required him to interfere. But when he tried to break it up, the two clung to each other like burrs, punching and kicking for all they were worth. He finally managed to pull a spitting and hissing Kyle off his brother.

Depositing the pint-sized warrior on the counter a good ten feet away from his brother, Jack turned and surveyed the damage. Noah had a swollen lip and a huge scratch down his neck, but looked otherwise unscathed.

The same could not be said for his kitchen.

Chocolate milk dripped from the walls, the floor, the table, the chandelier and even spattered the ceiling in a few spots. Crackers were scattered under the table, some ground into the tile while the plate of cheese remained relatively unscathed, except for the one random piece that was hanging on the wall.

He turned to the two boys, both of whom wore mutinous expressions. And both of whom had lower lips that trembled.

"Okay, so this snack thing was a little harder than I thought it would be," he told them. "My fault. I guess there's a learning curve for this kind of stuff."

"Are you gonna tell Mom?" Noah asked.

He raised an eyebrow. "Do I look like a snitch?"

"No." Both boys solemnly shook their heads.

"Okay, then. Let's get the mess cleaned up and then we'll try the whole snack thing again."

He grabbed the dustpan from the laundry room. "Noah, you're on cracker duty. Kyle, you're on milk duty on the floor, chairs and tables. I'll take care of the walls and ceiling. Sound good?"

The boys nodded, then Kyle pointed to the piece of cheese that was still hanging from the wall. "Who's on cheese duty?"

"Oh, I think I'm going to leave that there for a few days. A fitting memorial to the Battle of Chocolate Milk."

Noah laughed. "I could put another one up there for you. Then you could have two memorials."

Jack stopped, considered it for a second. "You know, that's not a bad idea." Then he held out the plate of cheese to Noah and said, "Fire away, soldier."

By the time Sophie was due to get the boys, Jack was physically and mentally exhausted. How did people do this? he wondered, yanking a shepherd's pie out of the oven where it had been heating up. How did they deal with two young children, filled to the brim with energy, and still find the wherewithal to go to work. He had a full shift in front of him and all he wanted to do right then was sleep.

But at least he, the boys and his house had all survived his first official day as babysitter, though it had been touch and go for a while there, especially with the house. On the plus side, he hadn't had time to sit down, let alone brood. So maybe there really had been a method to his madness.

With a sigh of complete and total exhaustion, he slid the shepherd's pie onto the table, tossed the salad, and sliced up a loaf of French bread.

Maybe he was being presumptuous, expecting Sophie and the boys to eat with him, but she could always say no. He figured since he had enough food to feed an army—neighbors in the South were so welcoming—and he had to eat anyway, he might as well feed them, as well. Otherwise, he'd be eating frozen dishes for the next year. And he wasn't even planning on sticking around here that long. If not back to Somalia, then to some other weather or war devastated country. Job security had never been a problem for him.

He sighed as he slumped into a chair and began to rub his aching leg. Kyle had gotten a few good kicks in before he'd managed to deposit him on the counter. He contemplated taking a pain pill, or at least some Advil. He knew, if he didn't, he'd end up suffering through his entire shift at the clinic and he really didn't want to do that.

He didn't want to move, either. The boys were in the next room, quietly playing on his computer—finally—and if he could just find five minutes to himself, he'd be back in fighting shape.

With a groan, he laid his head on the table and closed his eyes. All he needed was five minutes.

SOPHIE FOUND him fifteen minutes later, dead to the world, head resting on a dinner plate with his bad leg propped up on a chair, while the boys were playing some wizard game on the computer in the next room.

She burst out laughing. She couldn't help it. The big, bad surgeon looked so absurd passed out that way.

At the sound of her chuckling, Jack jolted upright and jumped to his feet, nearly upending the table in the process. "I'm not asleep," he told her blearily. "I was resting my eyes."

"Of course you were." She stepped forward, peeled a napkin off his cheek, then patted it. Poor baby, probably didn't know what had hit him. She'd tried to warn him.

"The boys are in the family room playing—"

She laid a finger on his lips to silence him. "I already found them. Thank you, for everything." She eyed the table. "We'll get out of your way so you can have dinner before work—"

"I thought we'd have dinner together." He gestured to the steaming shepherd's pie in the middle of the table. "I have enough food to feed an army."

"Ah, yes, is that one of the of the plethora of welcome dishes?"

"It is. I have about a hundred of them stacked in the freezer, so you'd be doing me a favor if you helped me out here."

She studied him for a second, then shifted her eyes to the dinner table to keep from showing her amusement. A week ago he'd been throwing out No Trespassing signs big enough to be seen in outer space and now he was inviting them all to dinner.

She wasn't sure what to attribute the change to. Maybe he was able to relax with her now that the difficult part—his injuries—was already out of the way. Or maybe he was a very private person who took time to warm up to people. Whatever it was, she liked these small peeks inside him. Oh, he wasn't letting her in very far, wasn't letting her near the dark torment that she knew was hiding deep in there. But at least he was showing her more than the stoic countenance he maintained for most people.

To make him sweat a little, and because he really was adorable in this sleepy, little boy lost way, she asked, "Is that Linda Grayson's shepherd pie?"

He blinked a few times, until the shadows of sleepy confusion cleared from his eyes. "Is Linda a tall blonde with generous—" he paused as she lifted an eyebrow at him "—tendencies?"

"Yes, Linda's *tendencies* are very generous," she told him. "As are her other assets."

"Then, yes, the casserole came from her."

"Linda must really be impressed. She doesn't make shepherd's pie for just anyone."

"Everyone in the neighborhood's been so nice. It's a big change from Boston." But, interestingly enough, reminded him a lot of Somalia, where the people were incredibly generous. They might not have had much, or anything, for that matter, but they were always willing to share.

Sophia snorted. He really was clueless. "That's because you're the hot new single doctor in town, Jack. They've been coming by to check you out." She stepped forward, patting his cheek for emphasis.

His eyes widened. "But most of them are married."

"Yes, but their husbands travel an awful lot. And some of them are over here, exploring the merchandise, not for themselves, but for their sisters or daughters or nieces or friends."

"The merchandise?" he repeated, obviously bemused.

She shook her head. "Southern women. They're a breed onto themselves."

"Interesting." He paused, considering her for a second. "How come I don't have a casserole from you?"

"Because I like you enough not to try to kill you.

And I've already fed you lasagna and homemade chocolate-chip cookies. What else do you want?"

He didn't say anything, but those amber eyes of his darkened while he looked at her. As they did, that strange little feeling came back, the one she'd been doing her best to ignore since the first time she laid eyes on him. When she thought something might happen, that he was going to say or do something—though she had no idea how she would feel if he did. But he looked away from her, at the table.

"So, do you want to stay?" he asked.

Her eyes darted to the clock over the pantry. "What time do you need to be at the clinic?"

"I've got to leave here in about half an hour. But that should be enough time, right?"

"Sure. Why don't you dish the food up while I get the boys washed up?"

"Sounds good."

It wasn't until a few minutes later, when she was settling herself at the kitchen table, that she looked up and saw two pieces of cheese hanging on the wall above Jack's head. When she pointed at them, he and the boys cracked up. And no matter how many times she asked throughout the rest of dinner, none of them would tell her why the hell there was cheese on the wall.

When they had finished eating, and as she watched Jack dart around the kitchen, grabbing his keys, wallet and other assorted things, she couldn't help admiring the way his hair stuck up in three different sections. That's when she decided she probably didn't want to know anyway.

Sometimes boys—and men—deserved their little secrets.

CHAPTER EIGHT

JACK WALKED HIS last patient of the night out of the clinic as Amanda bustled through the front door. "Hey, Stranger," she called to him.

He waved back, then headed to the small supply closet that now doubled as his office. It was right next to the one Amanda used for hers. He had a few charts he wanted to finish up and then he needed to get out of here. It was his second week on the night shift and though he'd spent much of his career working the 8 p.m. to 6 a.m. shift, this time around his body was having a difficult time getting used to it. Maybe it was because of the injuries or maybe it was because he was getting old. He was thirty-eight and though he'd never given a thought to his age before, since the shooting every day that passed seemed to weigh a little more heavily upon him.

Which was why he needed to get out of here. Some days it was all he could do to breathe in this place. The helpless, overwhelming feeling that he was suffocating slowly began to press in on him. Oh, Lucas and Amanda treated him like he was a contributing member of the staff, but the truth was, he was a long way from being able to pull his own weight and he was well aware of it. The fact that they pretended not to notice, and he pretended not to care, was even worse than the fact that he couldn't do for his patients all the things he wanted to.

He glanced at the clock. Six-twenty. Twenty minutes past quitting time. He tried to write faster, to finish the charts more quickly so he could go home and sleep, but it wasn't going to happen. These days, writing was a slow, painstaking, humbling experience if he wanted his penmanship to be even halfway legible.

As he reached for the second to last chart, he congratulated himself—he'd done a pretty good job of keeping up through the night. But still, he wanted to go home and catch a couple hours of sleep before the boys got home from school. It was Wednesday afternoon—which meant no homework—so they wanted to go to the park or maybe to an afternoon movie while Sophie finished up her court case. He was kind of hoping for the park, as the weather was supposed to be gorgeous, but something told him he was going to be outvoted in favor of the latest, outer-space robot movie. Kyle and Noah had talked about it nonstop all day yesterday.

When he'd volunteered to watch the boys until Sophie got a permanent sitter, he'd kind of thought he was doing them both a favor. In Sophie's case, she needed help and he could provide it, so why wouldn't he? And in his case, he figured his time with the boys would make his days go faster, which it did. But he'd spent the past couple of weeks trying to trick everyone—including himself—into believing that he was satisfied with this new life, but the fact of the matter was, he was barely interested in his existence let alone satisfied by it.

The time when he wasn't working or with the boys seemed to drag, and nothing, not even physical therapy for his hand and leg, could make it go faster. He was still missing something, though he wasn't yet sure what that something was.

Maybe it was For the Children—the pressures that came with running a hospital in war-torn Somalia were very different than the small irritations he faced working at an inner-city clinic in America. But maybe it was something else he wasn't quite ready to name.

All he knew was that working with Amanda again was both better, and worse, than anything he'd anticipated. Seeing her, touching her, smelling her every day, reminded him of how things used to be, before Gabby had died.

Before he'd watched her turn into a shell of the woman he loved.

Before he'd called Simon and watched as one of his closest friends healed—and then married—the only woman Jack had ever loved.

Was it any wonder he was a mess?

When Lucas had wanted to try dividing shifts up differently, in the name of efficiency, he'd jumped on the chance to take the night shift. Anything to get him away from constant, prolonged daily contact with Amanda and the glittering diamond ring and wedding band she wore on her left ring finger.

Taking over nights also left him free to be the boys' babysitter. What he hadn't counted was how much he would begin to enjoy their company. Noah was a whiz, super smart about all things science. He could spend hours regaling Kyle and Jack with little known facts that both amused and astounded them. Kyle, though only in kindergarten, was already a pretty impressive artist. Every day he drew fantastical pictures of a world only he could see, and then invited Jack and Noah and Sophie into it as he explained the pictures and all of the wild, mystical things to be found in them. Every refrigerator magnet he owned was currently being used to hold up Kyle's masterpieces. It had only been a week and a half but already he had to remember to stop at the store and pick up some new ones. If he couldn't display the latest pictures, Kyle would be crushed.

Even more unexpected than this pleasure was how much he enjoyed hanging out with Sophie for that hour after she got home from work. For the past few days, they'd sat outside, watching the boys play, swinging on the porch and talking about their days. Sophie was a good listener and so easy to be with that he found himself thinking about her more and more. Not in a romantic way—with a busted hand, a messed up leg, a career—and life—that was going nowhere, he so wasn't prime relationship material right now. But she was rapidly becoming a good friend. Someone he enjoyed hanging out and talking to about nothing more serious than the best way to garden in Atlanta's rocky soil or who was the biggest super villain of all time (though he did admit that that conversation had been heavily influenced by both Noah and Kyle).

"Knock, knock," Amanda said from the door. He beckoned her in as he continued to work on a chart. "I'm not sure I like this night shift thing for you," she said.

"Why not?" He glanced up, into her gleaming silver eyes, then forced himself to look away rapidly.

"I miss you on day shift. I was getting used to working with you again and then suddenly you were gone."

"Yes, well, there's only so much of me to go around," he teased.

"I've heard that," she answered, settling herself against the corner of his desk. "Lucky me that I finally caught up with you."

As she sat, she crossed her long legs out in front of her in the way she'd been doing since he first met her in the first year of med school. It was her thinking pose and seeing it now made him instantly wary. Combined with the contemplative expression on her lovely face, he knew without a doubt that she brought trouble waiting to happen.

"So, how are you doing?" she finally asked, holding a hand out to him.

"Fine, thanks." He eyed her hand curiously, but made no move to take it. He'd never been a masochist, except—of course—when he'd chosen to take this job. But that didn't mean he had to keep paying for the same decision over and over again. "Is there something I can do for you?"

"Obviously. I want to see your hand. How's it doing? Is it still healing well?"

"It's healing fine," he told her, impatient that so many of their conversations these days seemed to revolve around his injuries. Yes, he'd been wounded. Yes, it had sucked. But the fact of the matter was he'd survived. He didn't need her hovering over him every second like she was his mother. That had never been what he'd wanted from her.

She ignored the exasperation in his tone. "Well, then, let me see."

When he made no move to follow her orders, she rolled her eyes like he was a recalcitrant child she was having trouble dealing with, then grabbed his wrist. Her fingers were gentle as they caressed the scars on both the front and back of his hand. "Make a fist," she told him and he obeyed, simply because he figured giving in would get her away from him that much faster. He could smell her perfume and it was making him ache down deep inside where Amanda, thankfully, couldn't see.

"Good," she said, though he had yet to be able to

do much more than lightly curl his fingers toward his palm. "How's that feel?"

"Like I got shot three months ago," he finally snapped. "How's it supposed to feel?" He took an anxious sip of coffee.

She let his wrist fall to his side and smirked at him. "I was thinking more along the lines of 'like it's been run over by a semi—twice,' but whatever cranks your tractor, I suppose."

He choked. "Cranks my tractor?"

She pulled away, stuck her nose snootily in the air, and said "It's a Southernism."

"I guess so, because I guarantee you didn't pick that up in Boston...or Africa."

"Definitely not Africa," Amanda said with a laugh. But it was followed pretty quickly by a sigh as she grew more serious than he had seen her in quite some time. "Do you ever miss it?"

"Miss what? Somalia?"

She nodded.

No, he didn't. Which was weird—he was the first to admit that. He kept expecting to, kept telling himself that he should miss everything that he'd been doing there, but the sad truth was he didn't. Not really. Whether that was because of post-traumatic stress disorder or simply because he was worn out, he wasn't sure.

Either way, he wasn't in any kind of shape to tell the truth. So he lied, and refused to feel bad about it. "Yeah, of course. Don't you?" The last thing he wanted was Amanda's sympathy.

"I don't know. I dream about it sometimes, and the dreams are so vivid, so real, that sometimes I feel like I can reach out and touch them. Sometimes I wake up crying because I know I'll never be there again. Never have that same experience. It makes me sad even as I sometimes feel an overwhelming relief. Is that weird?"

He didn't think so, not when her description so completely summed up his own feelings. A beautiful dream followed by a nightmare of epic proportions, one that he was incredibly relieved to no longer be a part of.

Before he could say as much to Amanda, her eyes widened and she made a mad dash for the door. Alarmed, he followed behind her as she ran toward the restroom, barely making it inside before losing what sounded like the entire contents of her stomach.

He waited until she was finished, until he'd heard the toilet flush and the water running before going inside. "You okay?" he asked, wetting a paper towel and pressing it to her forehead as she clutched shakily at the sink.

"I don't know. That's the third time I've done that this week." Their eyes met in the mirror above the sink.

His heart broke a little at how scared she looked, how vulnerable, and yet how hopeful all at the same time. And that's when it hit him what a crappy friend he'd been lately. So wrapped up in his own feelings, his own misery, that he'd failed to see the abject fear lurking underneath Amanda's newly sunny exterior.

Had it all been an act? he wondered briefly. All that cheerful happiness as she worked to forge a new life out of the ashes of her old one? Had it all been as big an act as the one he was currently putting on?

If so, then he was a bigger jerk than he'd given himself credit for.

He ran a soothing hand down her back and asked softly, "Does Simon know?"

"I don't even know." Her laugh was shaky. "I've been too chicken to take the test."

"Because you want it to be true or because you don't?"

"A little of both, maybe?"

He nodded, understanding what she meant perfectly. Losing his career and trying to rebuild it had nearly killed him. He couldn't imagine what it would be like to lose a child as she had and then find out, two and a half years later, that you were expecting another one.

"You ready to find out for sure?"

"I don't know." The hand she pressed to her mouth was trembling as intensely as the rest of her.

He didn't answer, didn't move. Just waited for her to make the decision. When she took a deep breath and nodded, he excused himself, went to the cupboard where they kept the HCG strips and returned with one, along with a small container. He handed both to her and then stepped outside and closed the door to give her some privacy.

"Is Dr. Jacobs coming soon?" Lisa, one of the nurses, asked him. "The patients are stacking up."

"Which room is first?" he asked. "I can take a couple more patients before I head out."

He took care of a baby with Roseola and an older woman with pneumonia before the bathroom door finally opened. One look at Amanda's face told him everything he needed to know.

"When was your last period?" he asked, pulling her into an open exam room and reaching for the little chart that determined due dates.

She told him and he eyed her with surprise. It had been over two months. "I know. I wasn't ready to know."

He understood exactly what she meant. "It looks like you're going to be a mom again on or around June second."

Her eyes filled with tears and she nodded, right before she wrapped her arms around her middle and started to rock. He couldn't hold out against her obvious distress, and crouching down next to her, pulled her into his arms for a hug.

"I'm not replacing Gabby," she told him in a harsh whisper.

"Of course you aren't, sweetheart."

"I still miss her so much."

He nodded, then simply listened as she talked it out for the next few minutes. "I do want this baby," she told him eventually. "More than I ever thought I would."

"That's a good thing," he said, wiping a stray tear from her cheek.

"It really is." Finally, her face lit up with all the possibilities in front of her. "I need to tell Simon."

"Of course you do." He stood up, stepped back. "Why don't you go now? I can cover for you for a couple hours."

"But you've already worked a full shift!" Despite her protests, he could tell she was tempted.

"So? I'm not so old and decrepit I can't work a few extra hours on occasion. Go, do what you need to do and then come back."

"Thank you, Jack!" she squealed, throwing her arms around him and hugging him tightly.

"Hey, what are friends for?"

WHEN SOPHIE picked her boys up from Jack's house after work, she could tell something was wrong. The shell-shocked look was back in his eyes. The one she hadn't seen since that first night when he'd come to her house for dinner.

"Everything okay?" she asked, in between her boys' loud disagreement about the coolness level of the different robots in the movie Jack had taken them to that afternoon.

"Yeah, everything's fine."

"You sure?" she asked as she hustled her kids

out onto his porch. Maybe he simply needed some child-free time.

"Yeah. Hey, I know you have babysitting issues, but is there any way you can find someone to watch the boys Saturday night?"

Was he asking her out on a date? she wondered frantically. Out of nowhere? And if he was, what was she supposed to say? The last time she'd had a date it had been with her husband and she hadn't been in any hurry to jump back into the dating scene. Obviously. Jeff had been gone four years and she'd never found a man who interested her enough to consider going on a date.

And she still hadn't, she told herself firmly. Jack was turning into a great friend, but that didn't mean she wanted to muck that up by trying to turn their relationship into something it wasn't meant to be. Something she didn't want it to be, and something she sensed he didn't want it to be, either.

"Saturday night?" she asked cautiously, trying to get a feel for his weird mood—and the purpose of his inquiry. It was possible she was reading too much into the invitation.

"I'm supposed to have dinner with a colleague and her husband—we're celebrating her pregnancy. I thought, maybe, if you had a back-up sitter, you'd come with me. You know, as a friend? As a favor to me?"

"Oh, right. Of course." She felt her cheeks burning and hoped he didn't notice. She felt like an idiot for assuming, even for a second, that Jack was interested in her. "Well, let me call Elizabeth. She's a high schooler who lives down the street and sometimes sits for me. If she's available on Saturday, I would be more than happy to come with you."

"Great. Thanks." Was she imaging relief in the corners of his smile?

"No problem. And thanks for taking the boys to the movies. I was going to do it this weekend, but you saved me two hours of destructive, robot-on-robot fighting action. I appreciate it."

"I enjoyed it. So, anytime you want to escape from another boy flick, let me know. I'll be happy to take them again."

"Oh, you don't want to tell me that. I might be tempted to use you shamelessly."

As soon as she said the words, Sophie wanted desperately to recall them—and the totally unintended double entendre that came with them.

Jack's whiskey-colored eyes darkened a little in surprise and suddenly the air between them crackled with the beginnings of a sensual tension that she had never let herself recognize between them before.

Then again, she could be imagining it the same way she'd imagined that he had been about to ask her on a date. She didn't want to feel the fool again.

Lost in thought, she stepped back abruptly, and would have fallen off the porch if Jack hadn't caught her by wrapping his good hand around her elbow. The contact, though it was much more about steadying her than it was about any budding intimacy, made her even more uncomfortable. Made it difficult for her to breathe.

He didn't seem to be having the same problem, of course, which made her feel like an even bigger idiot than she already did. At least, until she looked up into Jack's eyes and saw, for the first time, an answering heat there. One that would be hot enough to blister her if she wasn't careful.

She might be woefully out of practice with all of this stuff, but that didn't mean she wasn't still aware enough to know when a man was thinking about sex. With her.

"Come on, Mom! I'm starving!" Noah's voice shattered the tension hanging in the air between them and she laughed nervously and shook her head slightly to clear the lingering uneasiness and desire.

"Go on ahead," she told the boy. "What time should I tell the sitter?" she asked Jack.

He cleared his throat, almost as if he was having as much trouble talking as she was. "Seven o'clock, okay?"

"Seven sounds perfect."

"Good." He opened his door, started to step back inside. Then paused long enough to say, "Thanks. I'm looking forward to going out with you."

"Me, too."

He bent and brushed a soft kiss across her cheek before closing the door behind him. She nearly sagged against the front of the house. If she was supposed to get through the next few days without desiring him, the last thing she needed was his mixed messages.

Didn't he realize things like that messed her up, not to mention got her into a tizzy about what to wear. Because if this was a date, then fine, she knew she needed to get dressed up, do her hair, put on a pretty dress. But if it wasn't, she didn't want to look like an idiot by dressing for something it wasn't. And if it wasn't, what was she supposed to do? Slide into jeans and a sweater?

Now that the question between them had been raised, it was excruciating. To Sophie, the torture was more proof that the whole dating scene wasn't for her. Which was fine, she decided, as she followed her boys home. Jack could call their Saturday night outing whatever he wanted but she was, very definitely, not calling it a date.

CHAPTER NINE

SHE ENDED UP going shopping for a new dress.

She knew it was stupid, knew it was unnecessary, was convinced that this thing between her and Jack was simply friendship. Yet she totally got suckered into it anyway. When it turned out that Elizabeth down the street couldn't babysit, she'd called her closest friend, Sabrina, to see if she was free.

Sabrina was, but in exchange for babysitting she wanted all the details. And halfway through Sophie's recitation of the facts, her friend had concluded that this was—indeed—a date. Casual, yes. Simply friends, maybe. But it was still the closest thing Sophie had come to social interaction with an adult of the opposite sex in far, far too long, so Sabrina was running with it as far and as fast as she could.

Which was how Sophie found herself sitting in the mall food court Thursday evening, sipping a latte while her two sons scarfed down hamburgers and French fries like it was their last meal. Seriously, she was going to have to see about those cooking classes. It appeared that boys really couldn't live on spaghetti alone...

"So, are you ready to find something spectacular?" Sabrina demanded, rubbing her hands together with glee.

"I wish you'd stop doing that. You look like some deranged fairy godmother."

"Excuse me if I think that you rejoining the land of the living is a thing to celebrate. You've buried yourself in work and the boys since Jeff died and it's more than time for you to start enjoying life again."

"I enjoy my life!" Sophie told her, a little indignant that her friend could think otherwise. "I have two children I adore, a job I love, and what I thought, up until a minute ago, was an awesome best friend."

Sabrina sighed—a larger than life, lingering sound that made Sophie smile despite the torture that was to come when she attempted to drag two little boys all over the mall.

"I am an awesome best friend," Sabrina insisted. "Which is why it's been so painful to sit by and watch as you struggled to get your footing these past few years. I know you loved Jeff very much, but you're a beautiful, vibrant woman. It's time for you to open up that part of yourself again."

It was Sophie's turn to sigh as she looked at her reflection in one of the mirrored columns that dominated the food-court décor. She didn't feel very vibrant right then, didn't feel very anything to tell the truth. Except tired.

She wasn't even going on an actual date and she was already exhausted by it. She'd tossed and turned for most of the night, which resulted in mega circles under her eyes that it looked like Kyle's black eye—which had finally healed—had moved over to her face in duplicate. Her hair looked dull, her skin looked duller, and there was a large part of her that wanted nothing more than to crawl back into bed and forget this whole day had even happened.

Sabrina would never allow such a thing, but it was a good fantasy. Especially considering the fact that she wasn't really sure how she felt about everything—neither the semi-date nor the shopping trip.

It wasn't that she didn't like the way Jack had asked her to accompany him—he'd been completely straightforward, just as a friend should be. No, what she didn't like was the way her heart had beat faster at the thought of going out with him. How, for one second, when she'd thought it was a date, she'd actually been excited. That's what she didn't like.

She had prickly defenses, she knew she did, and she'd honed them years ago as a foster kid with no one to depend on but herself. She'd allowed herself to loosen up with Jeff, to trust him and let him in a little bit. And then he had gotten killed. That should have proved to her the stupidity of opening herself up, of letting herself trust that someone else was going to be there for her.

But what scared her the most, what had her shaking in her hot pink tennis shoes, was the fact that she responded to Jack in a way she never had to Jeff.

She'd loved Jeff, in a sweet, almost abstract kind of way and had married him because he was a good man and she'd wanted a family—someplace where she belonged. But he'd never made her laugh the way Jack did, never touched her heart the way Jack did with his selfless determination to help others. They were just friends, but the fact that she thought about Jack as regularly as she did, and much more than her project required, concerned her a lot.

And then there was this shopping trip. She loved to shop as much as the next woman, but she liked to shop for herself. To please herself. This going out to find a dress to wow a man—it gave her a sickened feeling.

As a child, she'd gone on a million of these shopping trips through the years with different foster moms who squandered money over and over again in their efforts to catch men who only wanted them for one thing, or to keep men who had already lost interest in them. She'd sworn that she was never going to do that to herself or her children. And yet, here she was dragging her boys—who would much rather be at the park playing or at home riding bikes—along with her as she shopped for a dress and jewelry and maybe even a new pair of shoes.

She could tell herself she wasn't doing it for Jack. That she was doing it for Sabrina, or even better for herself. But there was a growing part of her that wanted to get a reaction from him. She was beginning to want Jack to look at her as something more than his pal next door. It was a stupid wish, and a frightening one, but it was there nonetheless. Pretending it wasn't was both cowardly and hypocritical.

In other words she was a mass of seething neuroses and it was only a matter of time before she cracked.

"I don't want to get hurt, Sabrina." The words came out of nowhere, but once she'd said them, she knew they were true.

"Oh, sweetie." Sabrina's eyes filled with sympathy. "Of course you don't. So take it slow. This is some kind of weird, half-date, so enjoy it. Get to know Jack a little more and see if you even like him—"

"I do like him. He's a great guy. Smart, funny, charming on the outside but with a million complex layers on the inside."

"He sounds perfect."

"Not at all. I mean, those layers, some of them are really dark."

"Mom!" Kyle interrupted. "I finished all my hamburger. Can I go ride on the tow truck?" He pointed to the fenced-in area with a half a dozen kiddie rides.

"As long as Noah goes with you." She reached into her purse and handed them each a dollar, enough for them both to ride twice. "And come straight back when you're done. Promise?"

"Promise!" Their little voices changed in unison. She watched them go, then turned back to Sabrina and their conversation about Jack. "I thought he was going to be my new project, you know?"

"What project is that? The get-Sophie-laid project?"

"No! Of course not!" She could feel herself blushing despite years of being exposed to Sabrina's blunt, over-the-top descriptions. "I mean, there's a lot of angst inside of him. It's hard to see, because he keeps up this charming façade with the world, one where he's funny and self-deprecating and sweet. But inside him there's a lot of anger, a lot of disappointment and confusion and even fear."

"You saw all this in a couple of weeks?" her friend asked, eyebrows arched in surprise. "He must be more relaxed around you than you think."

"Not necessarily. It's easy to see something in someone else when you live with it all the time in yourself."

Sabrina started to say something, but the boys picked that moment to return from the rides. Thank God. Sophie had already revealed too much and was feeling awfully uncomfortable about it. While it was true that Sabrina was her closest friend, that was a relative term. Because while Sophie would give her the shirt off her back without thinking twice, sharing her emotions was anathema to her.

"Are we ready to go shopping?" she asked brightly, taking hold of the boys' hands. The sooner she got this done, the sooner they could be on their way home. And right now, with more of her fears and feelings on display than she usually showed in a year, home seemed like a very good place to be.

She determined that when she was selecting a dress, she wasn't going to worry about what she thought Jack would like. She was going to pick one that she liked, that made her feel more vibrant and more alive, and that was going to be that.

It seemed a pretty tall order for one little dress, but she was going to give it a shot. Maybe she'd get lucky.

WHEN JACK got home from work on Friday—five hours later than he normally did, thanks to a massive accident one block away from the clinic that had sent a dozen injuries their way—he wanted nothing more than to grab a sandwich and stumble upstairs for eight straight hours of sleep. But since that wasn't going to happen—he was babysitting that afternoon—he'd settle for a three-hour nap.

But as he turned onto his street, he realized with some surprise that Sophie's SUV was parked in front of her house. Which was a strange place for it to be parked, even if he didn't take into account the fact that she was supposed to have had court until six that evening.

His surprise was even greater, though, when he turned into his own driveway and saw her on the porch in front of two beautiful Mexican pots, dark blue, large and happy looking. He'd been thinking about getting a pair ever since he'd moved in here.

He'd held off because he hadn't decided what he wanted to put in them, but Sophie had managed to do a fantastic job with them.

As he crossed the yard, he could see that each planter was filled with bright, beautiful flowers. Phlox and dahlias and geraniums in shades of red and yellow, with a little purple thrown in for good measure. It made him smile to look at them—and at her. The crappiness of his day quickly faded away as he bounded up the front porch stairs two at a time. It was a bit of a stretch for his leg, but he knew he'd never get any better if he didn't continue to push things every opportunity he got.

"To what do I owe all this?" he asked, settling into a crouch next to Sophie, who was sitting with her legs wrapped around one of the big planters as she patted down the soil. She was dressed in gray, low-slung yoga pants and a hot pink tank top that brought to mind all manner of inappropriate things. She was also covered in dirt.

"Court got out early today and instead of heading back to the office, I decided to stop by the nursery and get some fertilizer for our garden. While I was there, I saw those dahlias and they made me think of you." She looked up at him, a huge grin on her face. "After that, things kind of snowballed."

"Well, thank you. I've never had a woman bring me flowers before, let alone in such an imaginative way."

"That's me. If nothing else, I'm imaginative."

"Actually, I think you're quite a bit else," he told her, settling down next to her on the wooden boards of the porch. Since he had kissed her cheek a couple days ago, he had not been able to stop thinking about her. The kiss had been totally spontaneous, totally unexpected, and he had realized in the slow hours that had passed since he last saw her—totally sincere.

"Oh, yeah?" She lifted her face to look at him and he realized her nose was smeared with a streak of dirt. It made her look about sixteen, fresh and innocent and mischievous. "What else? Crazy?"

He leaned over, rubbed a finger along her nose until the dirt was gone. It didn't help much. She still looked fresh and— "Sweet."

"Yes, because that's how all women in their midthirties hope to be described. As sweet." He could practically hear the eye roll in her voice.

"Oh, yeah? How would you like to be described."

She did roll her eyes then. "Smart. Sophisticated. Sexy. Duh. Those are the good 'S' words."

"All right, then. You look smart, sophisticated, sexy."

"Thank you. But it doesn't count if I have to tell you to say it."

"I didn't think that was the kind of thing friends said to each other. Well, you didn't tell me to mean it. And I do. So that must count." He had the sudden urge to reach out and play with the hair that was curling with sweat on her neck. And for once, he didn't hold back.

Her hands stopped patting the soil and her spine straightened. His touch had made her as still as if she was listening to something emerge from deep within. Then, as though she'd gotten the answer she wanted, she grinned. "Yes, well I promise not to let the compliments go to my head. Somehow I'll keep myself from throwing you to the ground to have my wicked way with you."

Which was a shame, because he wouldn't mind having unrestricted, unclothed access to all those curves of hers. The thought came out of nowhere and grabbed him by the throat. "What? No response? Is the image so horrific it stole your voice?" When he still didn't answer, Sophie looked up from the planter. Their eyes met and the air between them crackled with the jolt of a sudden connection.

Before he could think better of the idea, he bent his head and touched her soft pink lips with his own.

Sophie froze for one long moment. He wasn't sure what to do, and was about to pull away when she turned and wrapped her arms around his neck, pulling him closer until his mouth fit fully over hers. Then she sucked his lower lip between her teeth and nibbled on it, even as her tongue soothed away the small, insignificant hurt.

The world around him started to spin and Jack pulled away for a second, tried to get his bearings, tried to make sure that this was what they both wanted. Sophie's eyes were still closed, and he couldn't help but run his good hand across her cheek. She moaned, a soft little whine in the back of her throat that told him everything he needed to know.

Lowering his head a second time, he pressed his mouth to hers. Once, twice, so soft and sweet that she felt like a rose petal against his lips.

Sophie moaned again, and this time her arms tightened around him as she pressed forward. It was his turn to groan, and he yanked her out from around the plant and into his lap, so that her breasts were pressed against his chest while her legs straddled his waist.

Then he was kissing her, really kissing her. He suddenly knew that this was what he had wanted all along, to be this close to her. His tongue delved into her mouth, probing and exploring. She felt like cotton candy dipped in sunshine. Like long summer walks along the Boston pier. Like everything fresh and light and wonderful and he couldn't get enough of her.

He pulled her body even closer, tilting her head so that he could tangle his tongue with hers and immerse himself in the perfect sweetness of the moment. He'd been in the cold dark for so long that he relished being wrapped up in her heat.

He felt her hands rise to his head and tangle in his hair and at first when she broke the kiss he thought she was going to push him away. But instead, she tilted her head back so he had perfect access to her throat and shifted to guide him closer.

The idea of tasting her neck, of feeling the smoothness of all that peaches and cream skin beneath his lips was a temptation he didn't even know how to resist. He skimmed his lips across her cheek to her ear then down her jaw to the sweet spot right behind her ear.

She jumped as he licked across it, then shuddered even as she pressed her body as tightly against his as she could get it. He moved from her ear to the pulse point at the hollow of her throat and began to lick.

SOPHIE WENT crazy at the feel of Jack's mouth touching and tasting her right in the center of her favorite erogenous zone. Heat, red-hot and electric, raced up her spine and she moaned as her body woke up with a vengeance from many years of hibernation.

He felt so good, made her feel so good, that she wanted to forget everything but this moment, forget everything but him and the way he felt—hands, mouth, body. She trembled at the way he fit against her, and at the thought of what he might feel like inside her. It had been a long time since she'd made love to a man, so long that she expected to be a nervous wreck at even the prospect of that kind of intimacy. But there was no room for nervousness here, no room for embarrassment as she clutched onto her friend's shoulders, onto Jack's shoulders, and felt herself opening to him in one luxurious stage after the other. He pulled away for a moment, though his breath was hot and heavy against her ear as he whispered, "Do you really want to do this?"

For a second, doubt—ice-cold and horrible—washed through her. "Don't you?" she whispered.

"Yes. Of course. I want—" When he literally choked on the desire behind his words, it was enough, more than enough, to drive away her doubt.

Twisting her fingers in his too-long hair, she yanked Jack's mouth back to hers and went about the slow, steady, fascinating job of devouring him. It was the most exciting thing that had ever happened to her. He smelled like sandalwood and lemon, tasted like coffee and rich dark chocolate, and she wanted to absorb him into her pores completely. To take him inside her and feel him in her every depth.

This time it was her turn to dip into his mouth, her tongue stroking over his, before moving on to the roof of his mouth. He groaned once more, his hands tightening in the hair that fell down her back. Then he wrenched his mouth away.

She tried to follow him, but he set her a little bit away from him. Not far, but just enough so that they both could think. In theory. "We can't do this here," he said through quick, heavy breaths. His voice was so husky with desire it was nearly unrecognizable. Reality came to her slowly.

"Oh, right." She remembered that they were sitting on his front porch, in full view of the entire neighborhood. But now that he'd been the voice of sanity, she didn't know what to do. Whether to suggest they go inside and pick up where they'd left off, or whether to go back to her planting like the past ten minutes had never happened.

She knew what she wanted to do, what her sex-starved libido was screaming at her to do. But that didn't mean Jack felt the same way. Obviously. He was the one who had called a halt to things. It was probably for the best anyway. She and Jack were friends, but sex complicated everything and it was a complication they both could do without. In fact—

Jack stood up, extending his good hand to her. "Do you want to go inside with me?" When she looked up at him in surprise, she realized that his eyes had darkened so much that the irises were nearly indistinguishable from the pupils.

Maybe she wasn't alone in these lust crazed feelings, after all.

And now that she looked closer, looked underneath her own desire, she could tell that Jack needed someone, needed her. His hands were shaking, his eyes were wild and he was on the verge of breaking apart.

Somewhere, in the back of her head, a voice was telling her all the reasons this was a really bad idea, that desperation sex never had a good outcome. But for once Sophie told the voice to shut the hell up. She was a grown woman walking into this thing with her eyes wide open. She knew Jack had issues right now, knew that she couldn't expect anything more from this than the pleasure Jack gave her. And she was okay with that.

Putting her hand in his, she let him pull her up and into the house.

THE SECOND the door closed behind them, he was on her, his arms wrapping around her even as he started backing her up across the room. She was on fire, her entire body going up in a conflagration of need that she couldn't escape. Didn't want to escape. It had been years since she'd felt this urgency, this passion—if, indeed, she had ever felt it—and she was going to revel in it as much as she could.

Jack's mouth raced frantically over her face. Over her forehead, down her cheeks, across her jaw before his lips finally found hers. When they did…when they did, her knees buckled and she had to twist her fingers in the soft cotton of his T-shirt to keep from falling. He was so intent on devouring her that she doubted he'd even noticed.

"I need to be inside you," he growled against her mouth, his hands slipping beneath her tank top to cup her breasts. They were full, aching, her nipples so tight it was a physical pain, and when his thumb brushed under her bra and against them she didn't know whether to scream in frustration or whimper with delight.

In the end she did both, letting out a sound that was as foreign to her as a one-night stand. The sound seemed to push him over the edge, because suddenly her yoga pants and panties were around her knees and he had two long fingers buried inside her.

She did scream then, the sensation of being full with him almost more than she could bear.

"I'm sorry," he growled, "I can't go slow. I'll make it up to you next time."

"Just do it," she whimpered. He reached into his back pocket and pulled out his wallet, yanked out a condom and tossed the rest across the room. He spun her around so that her bottom rested against his upper thighs, and as he tore open the wrapper, she braced her hands against the tall table he had in the entryway and bent at the waist in open invitation.

There was one long second of silence, one long moment of agony, while he sheathed himself and then he was there, between her legs. Blunt and hard and so big and thick that her eyes nearly crossed as he probed gently at the opening of her sex.

She expected him to be rough, hurried, expected it to even hurt a little at first as it had been years since she'd done this, and she braced herself for it. But now that he was so close, he didn't rush. Instead, he leaned forward until his lips were right next to her ear and whispered, "You're so beautiful. So damn beautiful." He ran his hand down her cheek.

The words, combined with the feel of him right against the core of her body ratcheted Sophie's need to a fever pitch. "Please," she begged. "I need—I need—"

"What?" he demanded, thrusting forward a little,

until he was buried about halfway inside her. "What do you need?"

Halfway wasn't enough.

"I need you!" she wailed, thrusting back against him.

That broke his control like a fragile, spring twig. Thank God.

He slammed into her so hard that he rocketed her up onto her toes. She was wet and hot and more than ready for him, so there was no pain—only pleasure so intense that she climaxed right there, with the first stroke of him deep inside her.

"Damn!" he growled, his fingers digging into her hips as he held her in place. Again, she expected him to pound into her, was even anticipating it, but he held her—and himself—still until she finished coming. As if he were absorbing every clench and contraction of her body on his.

As if he were somehow absorbing her very pleasure into himself.

Then he began to move again in slow, steady, powerful strokes that had her clutching at the table as the fire reignited deep inside of her. Soon—too soon—she was on the brink of coming again. But she didn't want to go over alone this time, didn't want to lose herself in the ecstasy without him.

Tightening her inner muscles in a long, slow caress, she did what she could to take him as high as he had taken her. He groaned and began thrusting harder, so she did it again. And again. And again.

His good hand worked its way up from her thigh to her hair and he pulled her head back sharply. She gasped, but didn't fight him as he twisted her head to the side.

"Kiss me," he commanded, seconds before his lips came down on hers, hard.

She did, pulling his lower lip between her teeth and nipping at him. She wanted more of him, wanted all of him. Craved him until he became an inferno in her blood.

She bit him again, a little harder this time, and the little shock of pain must have been what he was waiting for, because he came with a roar. She followed him over the edge, her body pulsating in twenty different directions as her orgasm ripped through her like a forest fire.

She wrenched her mouth from his, gasped for breath, but Jack wouldn't let her go. He followed her, his mouth ravenous on her own while the heat of his body seared hers wherever it touched. In moments, the pleasure swamped her, overwhelmed her.

She gave herself to him—to his kiss and his touch and the wild, wicked need that she had come to realize was as much a part of him as his caring heart and dark, wary eyes.

As she did, the whole crazy maelstrom started inside her all over again. She pulled him with her as she fell.

CHAPTER TEN

WHEN IT WAS over, when he was gasping for breath and it felt like his mind, his soul, his very essence had been sucked out of him and into Sophie, Jack gasped and slumped against her. He knew he needed to move, that he was pressing her upper thighs into the table, but for long seconds he couldn't do anything but rest against her soft, sweet body and try to recover.

He was still gasping, still dragging air into his oxygen-starved lungs, when she stirred beneath him. He forced his shaky knees to support him as he stepped back. "Did I hurt you?"

Now that he could see her face, the fear that he had indeed been too rough was livid inside of him. He'd taken her like an animal, he realized in vague horror. Had slammed her into the house and up against the furniture, had taken her from behind like a sex-crazed maniac. It wasn't how he would have wanted their first time to be.

Not that he'd spent a lot of time thinking about getting his new friend into bed, but if he had, he would have chosen something more romantic, less base and animalistic. If he'd been able to think or reason or do anything but want, he would have done it differently. But the second he'd put his mouth on Sophie's, it was like the entire world had faded away, until the only things left were the two of them and the almost violent need that stretched taut between them.

Stepping back even more, he prepared to apologize for his roughness, but his first look at Sophie's face stopped the apology in his throat.

She was glowing, her entire countenance alive with the power and passion of what they had done, and she was gorgeous with it. Oh, he'd always known she was a beautiful woman, but looking at her now, hair tousled, skin flushed, eyes more than a little sex-drunk, she was amazing. There was no sign of his sweet little neighbor, the one he'd felt the need to apologize to and coddle. Instead, she was a sex goddess, begging for another round.

He felt himself growing hard again and marveled at the wonder of it. Ever since he had been shot, he hadn't been particularly interested in sex, his libido tamped down by his physical and emotional pain. But it looked like he was making up for that in spades with sweet and sexy Sophie.

She noticed his renewed arousal, and her kiss-swollen lips curved in a knowing grin. "If you want to go a second round, you're going to have to feed me first. I'm starving."

He grinned, happy with her and himself and the whole world around him for the first time in a very long while. Shit. If he'd known making love to Sophie would do this to him, he would have tried to get in her pants a long time ago.

"What would you like?" he said, and after disposing of the condom he used his good hand to pull up his jeans and re-button them. It took him a lot longer than it would have three months ago, but Sophie didn't seem to mind. In fact, after she had rearranged her own clothing, she slipped behind him and copped a feel, her small, delicate hand tracing over the still aroused lines of his sex and making him even harder.

He blew out a long breath. "Are you sure you want to eat?"

"Positive," she answered as she moved past him into the kitchen. "I skipped breakfast this morning."

He wasn't sure what to expect when he followed her. Some awkwardness, probably, since this thing between them had come almost out of nowhere. Sure, he'd found her attractive, and obviously she had felt the same way, but he'd never really considered making love to Sophie before. He was still too fragile, though he hated to use that word, his mental outlook and peace of mind not what they needed to be to enter any kind of relationship.

But this didn't feel like a relationship, more like a friendship with really great benefits, and he certainly couldn't complain about that.

And she couldn't either, it turned out, because there was no awkwardness on her part as she rummaged through his refrigerator and came away with enough sandwich fixings to feed an army. "I can make you an omelet if you'd like," he told her as she laid out all the ingredients.

"Omelets take too long—to cook and to eat." She glanced archly at the clock. "I have plans for the three hours before the boys get home."

For the second time that day, all the blood in his head rushed south. "Let me help you with those sandwiches."

She laughed, a low, sexy sound he'd never heard from her before. He liked it. But then again, he was liking everything he found out about Sophie these days, even the stuff that had nothing to do with getting him laid.

As he spread mustard on a couple pieces of whole-grain bread, she reached back into the fridge and came out with a plate of homemade brownies. "From Melinda?" she asked archly, right before sinking her teeth into one. She moaned, then nodded. "Definitely from Melinda."

"Is Melinda a short brunette with big eyes?" he asked, to keep the game going.

"No. That's Jackie. Melinda is tall and gray-haired and I think the last time she smiled was sometime around the Reagan administration."

"Oh. Well those definitely aren't from her, then."

"Sure, they are. Jackie can't bake at all and certainly not like this. She must have conned Melinda into doing her dirty work."

"Hey," he said, stepping forward and taking a bite

of the brownie she held. "I object to being referred to as anyone's dirty work."

"Oh, yeah?" she asked, wrapping her arms around his neck and pulling him down for a kiss. "Does that objection extend to me, as well?"

He grinned against her mouth, loving the sweet, chocolatey taste of her. "Well, that depends what kind of dirty work you have in mind."

"The dirtiest."

"Oh, yeah?"

"Yeah." Her hands dropped to the waistband of his jeans and everything faded but his newfound need for her.

He stopped her before things went wild again, circling her wrists with his hands and gently pulling her away. "If you want something to eat, I suggest we focus on the sandwiches. Otherwise, I'm going to end up making love to you right here against these kitchen cabinets."

Her breath started coming in choppy little bursts. "Sandwiches are highly overrated," she told him breathlessly.

"You sure?"

"Absolutely. The brownies filled me up. Just don't tell Jackie about what became of her brownies or I'll get kicked off the neighborhood phone tree. Southern women are vicious about their baked goods."

"Is that so?"

"It is indeed."

"Well, then, my lips are sealed."

She grinned. "I really hope that's not the case." And then she stood up on tiptoes and pressed his mouth with her own.

As she'd teased him, Sophie's cheeks had turned a pale pink color that drove him wild, and the second her lips met his, Jack took control of the kiss, turning it into something that was both tender and ravenous. He wanted her—he couldn't believe how much he wanted her—and though he'd just had her, he felt, suddenly, like he could make love to her forever.

As her mouth met his, her tongue darting out to brush tentatively against his own, he told himself to take it slow this time. That they had all the time in the world. That there was no need to rush. The boys wouldn't be home for hours and after what had happened last time, he owed it to her to make this time last for longer than ten seconds. To make sure it was good for her.

Pulling away, he led her down the hallway to his bedroom, and the bed he hadn't bothered to make when he'd gotten up the day before. He laid her on the silky black sheets and then just looked at her for a minute, trying to etch every second, every memory, of this time deep into his brain so he could pull it out later and examine every nuance of it. Deep inside he knew that this thing between them wouldn't last long, that it might not even last until he went back to For the Children, but despite all that, despite everything that their separate futures held, this time with her was going to become one of his favorite memories.

Stretching out beside her, he reveled in the feel of all that soft skin and wild, sexy hair as it brushed against his body. Sophie was all woman—lush and round and so soft and fragrant that just a look, just a touch, brought him right up to the edge of his control. And when she leaned forward, brushed his lips with hers, he hardened to the point of insanity.

"Do you have any idea how much I want you?" he asked, cupping the back of her head to keep her lips against his.

"I think I've got a pretty good idea after our performance down in the foyer," she answered, her tongue licking across his bottom lip.

"Don't bet on it." His hands tightened in her hair, pulling her closer to him, so that he could delve inside her mouth like he so desperately wanted to.

Sophie nearly went into sensory overload when Jack's mouth crushed against hers. It felt so good to be held by him, kissed by him—a part of her wanted to crawl into his lap and never, ever let him go.

Of course, she knew that wasn't practical—despite how close she felt to him right now, despite the fact that he was the only man she could imagine giving up her long-held control to—she barely knew him. And what she did know of him did not lead her to believe that he was the happily ever after type.

Not that she expected him to be, or even wanted

him to be. But when he held her and kissed her, he tasted like forever and things got all mixed up in her head. But she could deal with all that later, she told herself. Right now she wanted nothing more than to rub herself against him and take everything, anything, that he wanted to give her.

Jack chose that moment to nip at her lower lip and as she gasped every thought she had melted into oblivion. She could think later, reason later, right now all she wanted to do was feel.

He nipped at her again and she parted her lips for him, let him slide his tongue deep inside her. He stroked his tongue against hers, circled hers, before beginning a series of slow in and out movements that made her crazy. She moved to meet him, thrust for thrust.

When she returned his motions, he groaned, low and deep. Delight streamed through her at this proof that he really was as affected by her as she was by him. That this smart, selfless, sexy man really wanted her as much as she wanted him.

Thrusting her tongue into his mouth, she toyed with him. Slipped and slid against him with glancing touches. Played with him. Teased him. Tormented him as she pulled the flavor of him deep inside her.

He broke away with a groan, rolling onto his back. His chest rose and fell rapidly while his hands fisted the sheets.

She knew he was struggling for control, but she had no intention of letting him regain it. She wanted to make him crazy, wanted to bring him the same insane pleasure that he brought her.

"Careful," he said as she lowered her mouth to his beautiful chest and began licking over the slick muscles there. "I'm afraid I'm going to lose it like some fifteen-year-old kid with his first girl if you keep that up."

She grinned, liking the sound of that. "That's more than okay with me."

"Yeah, well, not for me. I'm trying to take this slow, but when you look at me like that all I can think about is getting inside that hot little body of yours and taking you until you scream from the pleasure."

Her whole body burned at his words, her nipples tightening so fast that they actually hurt. "I don't think I'm a screamer. Or at least, I never have been before."

He rolled over so that she was buried beneath his rock-hard body, though he kept most of his weight balanced on his elbows. "Let's see what we can do about that."

Lowering his head, Jack took her mouth in what he intended to be a sweet, gentle kiss.

A slow, controlled kiss.

A kiss that would slowly stoke the fire between them until Sophie forgot everything but him, everything but the fire they built together.

Or at least, that's what he intended. But the second her arms locked around his neck, he was once again lost in her. The pleasure wrapped around him, took him over, the taste and scent and silken feel of her taking him right up to the brink of his control all over again. He couldn't move without wanting her, couldn't breathe without needing to be all the way inside her. He was on fire and the only way to survive was to plunge himself inside her until they burned with a single flame.

He was shaking by the time he lifted his lips from hers to trail wet, open-mouthed kisses across her cheek to the sensitive skin behind her ear. He dallied there for a moment, teasing her, just for the pleasure of hearing her gasp and moan. And then he was moving on, down the long, slender column of her neck and the sweet curve of her shoulder.

He nipped and kissed, licked and sucked his way down her arm. Paused at her wrist and flicked his tongue back and forth over her rapid pulse before moving on to her mound of Venus, the strong fleshy pad at the base of her thumb. It was one of his favorite parts of a woman and he spent a couple minutes kissing it before sinking his teeth into it in one quick bite.

She cried out, jerked against him, while her free hand clutched at his hair. Loving the feel of her long, slender fingers scraping against his scalp, he laved the small hurt he had inflicted with his tongue until he was sure that the sting had dissipated. Then he pressed a kiss right to the center of her palm, savoring her soft, supple skin and the sweet lilac scent of her.

She moaned a little, so he lingered, gently licking the spot he'd kissed until she cried his name on a broken breath. God, he loved the way that sounded. Loved knowing that he was bringing her pleasure and, in some heretofore unexplored caveman part of him, loved knowing that it had been a long, long time since another man had heard her make those sounds.

Reaching up, he pulled her hand from his hair and started all over again on the left side.

SHE WAS LOSING her mind. There was no other explanation for the fact that she felt hot yet cold, fragile yet strong, drained yet so filled with electricity that she figured she could power half of Atlanta for a week. She couldn't breathe, couldn't think, couldn't do anything but feel as Jack took her apart one slow kiss at a time.

She'd never known anyone could be so patient, never knew anyone could be so thorough. Jeff had been a good lover, considerate and kind, but he'd never taken this kind of time with her. Never brought her right to the brink of orgasm again and again and again without ever letting her go over.

It was like Jack had all day, like the huge, hot erection she felt against her leg didn't matter to him. Like she was the only thing that mattered. She couldn't imagine what he found so fascinating about her responses, but she wouldn't trade this pleasure for the world.

As he licked his way over the bend of her arm,

pausing to nibble at her elbow, she wondered if there was any part of her body he didn't plan to kiss or lick or caress. Or if he was going to spend all afternoon driving her to the brink of insanity and then beyond.

She wanted to touch him, wanted to explore the hard, male body she had been admiring since the first time she laid eyes on him. Wanted to run her hands over the strong muscles of his back, to cup the fabulous behind that had worked its way into her fantasies more than once in the past few weeks.

Finally, finally, he finished with her arms. As soon as he let her go, she wrapped herself around him and pulled him down to her, so that she could explore the taste of him, as well. But he was having none of it. She'd only gotten one quick taste of him—a long swipe of his collarbone—before he was pushing himself off of her. "None of that, sweetheart," he said with a rakish grin that shot heat straight to her sex.

"But I want to touch you, too."

"You have. You are." He softened the rejection with the brush of his lips over hers. "I'm too close to losing control."

"It doesn't feel like you're too close. You're torturing me."

"I'm making love to you, Sophie. That's not even close to torture."

"Easy for you to say," she grumbled, a little shocked at how whiny and out-of-sorts she sounded. But damn it, she was beginning to think he was never going to make love to her. That first time, in the entryway, seemed like a hundred years away and her body was achy, needy, desperate to feel him inside her again. "I'm going to explode at any second."

He grinned. "And I've barely gotten started."

"You can't mean that. I'm going to die if you leave me like this."

"Don't worry about it. I know CPR." He shifted so that his mouth was on the same level as her abdomen.

"Funny." She had more to say to him, but then he circled her navel with his tongue and she forgot how to speak. His hands came up, cupped her breasts, moved in the same gentle circles as his tongue. She arched her back, tried to get him to press harder, to go faster, but he was having none of it. He was determined to drag this out until she really did have a heart attack.

His mouth skimmed across her stomach, pressing kisses up one side of her rib cage and down the other. His tongue darted out, stroked the sensitive skin between each of her ribs before licking a long, straight trail from her navel to her collarbone.

Fire bloomed inside her wherever he touched, burned across her skin before sinking in to the flesh below as he delivered a series of small, stinging kisses. She cried out, clutched at his hair, but he only laughed. It was a low, wicked sound that wrapped itself around her nerve endings and took her even higher.

When she was on the brink of screaming, crying, begging, he brushed his mouth over her nipple, darted his tongue out and licked her before blowing a slow, steady stream of air across the aching bud.

She did scream then, her breathing coming faster and faster as she waited for him to do it again. He made her wait, one second, two, and then his mouth was on her. His hand kneaded her breast as he sucked her nipple deep into his mouth and then nipped at her, using his teeth and tongue to sting and soothe and deliver more pleasure than she'd ever dreamed possible.

Jack moved from one breast to the other, one nipple to the other, sucking her hard one second and then barely touching her the next. She never knew what he was going to do, never knew what kind of pleasure to expect, and it kept her on the edge of a precipice even as it took her higher and higher and higher.

And then he was shifting again, kissing his way down her breasts as his hands moved over her abdomen and then lower, his fingers dancing over her mons and the soft curls there.

"Open your legs for me, Sophie," he murmured, his voice low and deep and sexier than she had ever heard it.

For the first time since they'd started this, nerves assailed her. Her thighs trembled as she tried to work up the nerve to open herself to him completely, to let him into this most sensitive, private place. The only man to ever do this to her had been Jeff and even then, not until they'd been together for a while and not all that often. The idea of doing it with Jack now…it was a lot to wrap her head around.

"What's wrong?" he asked when she continued to hesitate. He didn't rush her, didn't try to coerce her, didn't grab on to her thighs and open her himself. He simply waited, his mind and body completely attuned to hers.

Slowly, so slowly she wasn't sure she was even doing it, she spread her thighs apart. Then held her breath and waited as his gaze shifted from her face to her sex. He didn't touch, didn't race to the prize, just spent long, leisurely seconds looking his fill. Her thighs were trembling and her heart was beating way too fast by the time he reached a single finger toward her and began to stroke.

"You're so beautiful here," he said, and it was almost a growl. "So pink and soft and beautiful that it hurts to look at you. I want to be inside you so damn badly that I'm about to lose my mind."

They weren't love words, but they were real and honest and so sexy that she felt herself surrender once and for all.

"Take me," she begged arching to meet his finger. "Please, Jack, I need you so badly that it hurts. Please make love to me. Please."

He groaned, then lowered his head so that his tongue could replace his finger on her soft, slick folds.

She jumped at the unexpectedness of the caress, then melted as he swiped his tongue over her labia a second and then a third time. It felt nothing like she'd ever imagined, nothing like she'd ever dreamed about. It was hotter, wetter, sexier, and more pleasurable than she might ever have guessed it could be.

Lifting her head to look at him, to watch him as he went down on her, she was shocked by the intensity of his gaze, by the dark and wicked sensuality of his face. He was as wrapped up in her as she was in him, his entire focus on the fire the two of them were building.

Then he pressed his face against her sex, inhaled, his fingers shifting lower, clamping down on her thighs to hold them open for him, and he thrust his tongue deep inside her. She screamed and bucked beneath him, her hands tangling in his hair as she stared blindly at the ceiling.

And then he began to move, his tongue driving into her again and again, stroking her pussy from the inside as he stoked the flame inside her to fever pitch. He was devouring her, swamping her, taking her to a place where there was no time, no problems, nothing but pure sensation.

When she couldn't take it anymore, when her body was on the brink of shattering into a million irretrievable pieces, he stopped. Withdrew. And his tongue went from driving deep to fluttering silkily.

As his tongue clicked back and forth across her clit, he slid one finger from his good hand inside her slowly. Then he bent that finger a little, so that it pressed against the front wall of her vagina and she shattered.

There was no slow build-up to orgasm, no gently increasing tension. She exploded as pleasure, white-hot and unbearable, poured through her.

"Sophie," Jack groaned even as he slid a second finger into her. "You feel amazing. I could stay here forever making you come over and over again and die a very happy man."

She licked her lips, tried to talk, but her voice was broken, her ability to breathe nearly gone. She was simply lost in sensation, the rhythmic contractions inside of her stealing everything from her but the pleasure.

Before they could ebb, he was at it again, licking and sucking at her clit until the tension bloomed hotter than ever, the sensations building and crashing continually. He hurtled her into another orgasm and then another one, his mouth moving over and against her until there wasn't a part of her body that wasn't on fire. Her breasts ached, her nipples burned, her arms and legs and stomach and back felt so sensitive that even the air acted as a stimulant.

"Stop," she gasped. "Please, Jack, you have to stop. I can't take this."

"You can take it," he growled against her. "You can take this and more, Sophie. You can take everything I want to give you."

HER BREATH was seesawing in and out of her lungs, and hot tears of pleasure, of surrender, were leaking out of her eyes, and still he needed to drive her higher. Still he didn't stop. He couldn't. Making her come, watching her flush and writhe and moan, was one of the most sublime experiences of his life.

He was so hard he really thought he was going to explode. Every sound she made shot right through him until the act of breathing was agony. He was so sensitive that even the silky fabric of the sheets hurt and he knew if he didn't get some relief he was going to go insane.

And still he couldn't bring himself to stop touching her, kissing her, licking her. He wanted to make this good for her, needed to make sure that no matter what happened in the future—she would remember these moments between them.

"Jack, you have to stop. You have to stop." She was crying out in earnest now, the pleasure so overwhelming that everything else had ceased to exist. Which was what he'd wanted, what he'd needed—her so lost in the pleasure that when he did take her she would remember only how good it felt to have him inside of her.

Keeping his fingers deep inside her, he slid up her body slowly, delivering kisses on every body part he could reach before he finally claimed her mouth. Her hand came up to cup his cheek and he melted a little as her fingers stroked tenderly.

"Are you ready?" he asked hoarsely.

"Yes!" Her hips bumped against his. "Yes, Jack. Yes, yes, yes!"

"Then kiss me again."

He slid deep with one thrust of his hips and she screamed a little, then whimpered.

"Are you okay?" he demanded, ripping his mouth from hers.

She didn't answer. Her head was thrashing back and forth against the pillow while her hands clutched at his hips and her body shuddered underneath his. "Sophie?" he asked again, the feel of her rippling around him taking him all the way to the edge of his control. He was going to lose it soon, lose it quickly, and he needed to make sure she was okay. "Sophie, answer me!"

"Do it!" she cried, her nails digging into his back. "Do it, Jack. You're killing me!"

Her words were all the answer he needed and he pulled out slowly before thrusting back in again and again, each time faster and harder than the one before it until both he and Sophie were on the edge of orgasm.

Her hands were all over him, racing over his back, clutching at his ass, tangling in his hair as her hips moved beneath his with more and more surety. She felt amazing, tight and hot and so slick that he could barely breathe. He was close, so close that he swore the top of his head was going to blow off when he finally allowed himself to come, but he was determined to bring her with him.

Moving his hand between them again, he rubbed against her at the same time he told her, "Let go,

Sophie." His voice was so low and guttural he barely recognized it. "Let me feel you, sweetheart."

She gasped, wrapped her legs around his upper thighs and pistoned her hips against his. His eyes crossed, his breath held in his chest and his restraint shattered. Grabbing her hips, he thrust himself inside her hard. She screamed and started coming. The rhythmic contractions set him off, his orgasm roaring through him like an engine letting off steam.

Sophie clutched at his shoulders, and pulled him down on top of her. He let her, and as her hard nipples brushed against his chest, he gave himself over to his release and came and came and came.

CHAPTER ELEVEN

AFTER SHE'D STOPPED trembling in the aftermath, Sophie lay in bed and waited for her heartbeat to slow. Wow. Just wow. She'd known Jack was a generous guy, but never in her life would she have imagined he would be a lover like that. Her body, and her heart, might never recover.

Admittedly, she'd only had one real lover in her life, Jeff, and he'd been a caring, wonderful husband. But he hadn't rocked her body the way Jack had, hadn't made her forget everything but the two of them and the amazing things he was doing to her . As for the boys she'd slept with when she was young and stupid, looking for someone, anyone, to love her—they weren't even in the same galaxy. Of course, she barely remembered any of their names or what they looked like, while she had a feeling she'd never be able to forget anything about Jack.

Rolling onto her side, she studied him. Exhausted from working a shift and a half at the clinic, he had passed out almost as soon as he'd rolled off her. Which was fine with her, more than fine, because it gave her a chance to observe him unaware.

He looked different asleep, when the charming—but guarded—façade dropped away and revealed what was really going on inside him. It wasn't exactly a sight that comforted Sophie. Instead of looking relaxed or carefree when he slept, he looked miserable. Tortured. And about five years older.

Here, now, in bed with her, the pain he managed to keep hidden when he was awake was written plainly on his face—in the deep grooves around his mouth and the lines of worry and sadness that were etched around his eyes. This was the real Jack, the one he hid from everyone, even her. Especially her. After that first night at her house, when she'd pushed him too far, too fast, he'd been extra-careful to hide his torment from her.

He was still handsome, though. Maybe even more beautiful, as she had never been one to fall for perfection—in art or in life. She liked the character lines in his face, liked the character behind them, as well. Jack was one man in a million. One who gave selflessly of himself even though he didn't have to. One who always found a way to make her day better, no matter how miserable he was.

What did that do to him? she wondered. What was it like to keep everything bottled up inside of you because it was the only way you knew to protect yourself and those around you? She knew something about that, but there were places she relaxed, people she relaxed with. She might not wear her heart on her sleeve, but at least she had some kind of outlet.

She didn't claim to know everything about Jack, but she understood enough to see that he was locked down so tightly it was a miracle he didn't explode. Or implode, because that was the type he was. He held it all inside until he couldn't breathe anymore. Couldn't function.

Maybe that's why he made love the way he did. So powerful, so focused, so passionate that she felt like she'd been scorched. If she'd given any thought to what it would be like to sleep with Jack—and maybe she had, a little—she would have expected making love to him to be sweet, fun, exciting. But this... She sighed. This had been so much more. This had been soul-searing, overwhelming, so much so that she still wasn't sure how she was going to face him when he woke up.

She felt like he'd broken her protective shell open, and everything inside of her—everything she kept private—was now on display. She didn't like it, though she had to admit that she already craved a repeat performance of this afternoon's antics.

Too bad she had no idea how to deal with it. Oh, she knew this didn't change things between them. It's not like they were dating or anything like that. They were friends who had an undercurrent of attraction running through their relationship, which—for whatever reason—had burst into flames today. She didn't know what had caused it, but she was smart enough to know it wasn't her and her flowers.

No, what had happened between them had come

from Jack. Something had caused all the emotions simmering inside of him to pop and she had simply been there. The most unbelievable sex of her life had been the result. She hoped that whatever it was that had set him off had somehow been released, or at least relieved, by what they'd done together. For his sake.

Her stomach growled—such a mundane thing to have happen while she was contemplating the weight of the universe—and she glanced at the clock. She'd spent over two hours in Jack's bed, which meant she had about half an hour or so before the boys got home from school. Just enough time to take a quick shower and, if she was lucky, finish up the pots outside.

But when she started to get up, Jack's arm snaked around her waist and pulled her against him. She started to laugh, to explain her reasoning to him, but when she rolled over to face him, she realized he was still asleep.

There really was a lot going on under the surface there, she thought, brushing a soft kiss across Jack's forehead before slowly disengaging his arm. She wished she knew what it all meant. Were they still friends? Friends with benefits? Or were they moving into lover territory? And if they were, how exactly did she feel about that? She wasn't sure, but she'd better figure it out pretty quickly. Because if she knew Jack, once he woke up, he was going to be right back in her face—one way or the other.

JACK CAME TO awareness slowly. Rolling over onto his back, he stretched his cramped muscles and smiled. He hadn't slept like that for a long time, dead to the world around him. But when he reached out a hand to touch Sophie, he was alarmed to realize she wasn't there with him. He glanced at the clock, and when he saw that it was almost seven, he sat straight upright. Night had crept across the sky and the room was filled with shadow. He was only working a half shift tonight—it started at eleven, but still. He'd slept a large portion of the day away. Thank God Sophie had been home to get the boys today as he had totally fallen down on the job.

What a jerk. He'd come home while Sophie was doing something nice for him, had practically assaulted her on his front porch, then dragged her inside and made love to her until he was nearly in a coma. And hadn't even checked with her to make sure she was on kid-duty today. Totally smooth.

What must she be thinking? he wondered as he rolled out of bed. What was he thinking, for that matter? Sophie was his friend. Yes, she was beautiful and yes, he was attracted to her, but she was his friend. And he had all but attacked her.

When he thought back to what he'd done to her, what they'd done together, his stomach nose-dived. After losing a patient that morning, he'd been walking a fine line of control as it was. And then he'd come home and seen her and all the emotions he tried so hard not to feel had rushed up, exploding outward.

He'd pushed Sophie hard, had taken everything she had to give as he demanded reactions from her that were more in line with long-time lovers. And it had only been their first time together. Sure, it had been amazing. Unbelievable, and so exciting that he was getting aroused thinking about the long, passionate minutes. But still. He'd given her no reassurances. He told himself that it was because he had nothing to give, but that didn't excuse him. Sophie wasn't the kind of woman who indulged in one-night stands. And yet that was exactly how he'd treated her, rolling over and going to sleep without so much as a few sweet words. Forget jerk. He'd been a total Neanderthal.

No wonder she was long gone.

Annoyed beyond measure, Jack rolled out of bed and headed straight for the shower. As he did, he winced a little at all the small muscles that twinged after hours of intense lovemaking. It was a good wince, and they were good pains, but still, he was a little embarrassed. He was always an intense lover, but never had he pushed a woman like he had Sophie. So quickly and so completely. He'd sensed her holding back at the beginning and it had snapped something deep inside of him. They weren't together, but he liked her, admired her. Trusted her in a way he didn't trust many people. He wanted that same trust from her and had pushed at her until he'd gotten it.

He wanted to feel bad, and if he was honest with himself, he did feel like he'd gone at her too hard. But at the same time, he loved the way she'd handled it. Loved the sex they'd had. It was amazing his house was still standing.

He took a super fast shower, then got dressed almost as quickly. Maybe Sophie had left because she wanted some time to process what had happened. Maybe she had left simply because she'd needed to be at home with her kids—though he didn't get that because they crashed at his house all the time. Whatever the reason was, he was going to get it out of her. The gentlemanly thing might be to wait until she came to him, but he knew that wasn't going to happen. If Sophie had run, or even retreated, he was going to have to be the one to go over there. Which he would, gladly, as long as it didn't mean having to define their relationship.

He didn't want to do that right now, didn't even know if he could. He liked Sophie, loved spending time with her and her kids. But at the same time it felt like he had fast-forwarded through a bunch of steps, skipping many steps that might actually help them both make sense of what was between them. He wasn't sure what to do about that.

But he had to do something. Sophie deserved it.

WHEN THE doorbell rang at five after seven, Sophie wasn't the least bit surprised. As the boys ran for the door, scrambling over each other in their determination to reach it first, she tried to decide what she was going to say to Jack. Nothing came to her, but then, she wasn't surprised after four hours of thinking in useless circles about how she wanted this meeting to go.

Kyle won the battle, with a little strategic help from her, since Noah had totally been cheating. God love her firstborn, he had a no-holds-barred attitude about competition and it was going to end up getting him in trouble someday.

Kyle flung the door open and Jack stood there, hands shoved into the back pockets of his worn jeans with a look on his face that was halfway between guilt and satisfaction. She knew exactly how he felt, only she was leaning—heavily—toward the satisfaction portion of the equation. She hoped by the time he left here, he would be, too.

"You busy?" he asked from his side of the threshold.

"Not at all. Come on in. The boys and I were about to break out superhero Yahtzee, if you'd like to play with us."

"Oh." He looked distinctly uncomfortable. "Sure. Have you eaten already?"

"We did, yes, but I've got leftovers if you'd like."

"That would be great, thanks," he said, all good manners and politeness. It made her want to giggle like a schoolgirl—nerves always did that to her—but really, of all the reactions he could have had, politeness wasn't a bad one.

"Noah. Kyle. Get the game set up and sharpen four pencils so we can each have our own. There's a new box upstairs in the top drawer of my desk." Satisfied that would keep them busy, at least for a little while, she turned back to Jack. "Come on," she told him, leading the way to the kitchen. "It's just spaghetti, but there's plenty of it."

He laughed. "Mama Maria strikes again."

"She does, indeed. But at least it's healthier than takeout."

"You know, I could teach you how to cook a few more dishes, if you'd like."

"You know how to cook?"

"You say that like it's such a shock."

"No, I just haven't seen you do it once in all the days I've picked the boys up at your house."

"I said I know how to cook, not that I love it so much that I'd do it when I still have a house full of casseroles."

"Oh, right. I'd forgotten about the parade-of-casseroles."

"Does that ever get old, by the way? When does the welcome wagon in the South decide that enough is enough?"

"Right around the time the handsome single doctor decides to get married."

Oh, God. Sophie froze the second the words left her mouth. Had she really just said it? It was the truth, but maybe too much of the truth for this exact moment? Now Jack probably thought she was angling to go from one afternoon in his bed straight to the altar—which couldn't be further from the truth.

She could feel her cheeks start to flame—damn redheaded complexion—and ducked her head into the refrigerator in an effort to cool them down. And avoid his gaze, but Jack didn't need to know that. She rummaged in the refrigerator, pretending to search for the spaghetti as she waited for him to run for the hills.

But thank God Jake didn't freak out as easily as she did, because he laughed.

He said, "The flowers look great. Thanks so much for doing that for me."

"They do, don't they? I'm so glad you like them. I was worried when I put the purple in that you'd freak out. Phlox isn't what one would exactly call a manly flower. But I thought it was a nice foil to the hot colors of the others." It was her turn to laugh as she realized how absurd they both sounded.

Turning to face him, she asked, "Are we really standing here talking about flowers?"

Jack considered this for a second. "It would seem that we are."

"Why?"

"Because we don't want to talk about the fact that we spent the afternoon having the best sex of our lives?" he suggested. Then paled a little. "Or, at least I did."

It was the first time his composure had faltered since he came to her door, and it helped her to relax a little bit. Reminded her that he was still human and that she wasn't alone in this. "I did, too," she rushed to assure him.

Jack didn't say anything for long seconds, so Sophie busied herself getting his plate in the microwave. "Lemonade?" she asked, reaching for a glass.

"What? Oh, yeah, that's fine. Look, Sophie…"

Ugh. The part of herself that had been holding its breath ever since she'd crawled out of his bed that afternoon exhaled on a huge sigh. So it was to be one of those discussions, the kind that started with "Look," and ended with a broken heart. Except her heart wasn't going to be broken. It wasn't even going to be bruised. She'd made sure of that in the hours since she left his bed.

Sure, she had reasoned, Jack was the first guy she'd been with since Jeff had left for Afghanistan five years ago, but she wasn't expecting any kind of commitment from him. They were just friends, after all. Neighbors. They'd both been lonely this afternoon and whatever had happened had happened. That was it.

But judging from the look on Jack's face, he wasn't thinking the same way she was. But then how could he be? She was the one who'd brought up marriage, no matter how innocuously. He probably thought she was picking out china patterns in her head. Which meant there was nothing else to do but brazen it out.

"Uh-oh," she said, depositing Jack's plate on the

table in front of him before handing him a napkin and a fork. "Someone has his serious face on."

Jack grimaced and her hands began shaking so much that she shoved them in her pockets. Judging from the look on his face, this was going to be even worse than she'd anticipated. Determined to postpone the inevitable, she gave him a breezy smile and said, "Don't worry about it, Jack. It's fine."

His eyebrows drew together, though she wasn't sure if it was a result of her words or her tone. "What's fine?" he demanded.

"You know. What happened earlier. It was no big deal, right. Just chemistry or hormones. Whatever you want to call it. But it was fun, right? We both had a good time? Let's leave it at that."

Underneath the already furrowed brow, his eyes grew stormy. "Did you really blame making love to me on hormones?" he said. "We're not sixteen, Sophie."

She couldn't believe how blunt he was being. No euphemisms from the good doctor, rather a lot of facts bundled together like a question. She wanted to think, wanted to be alone for a few seconds so she could figure out what she was supposed to say. But the look on Jack's face told her that that wasn't going to happen. Nothing was, until they settled what was between them.

Deciding if he was going to be blunt, she could be brazen, so she winked at him. "No, we're not. But I am thirty-five, and you know what they say."

Now those whiskey colored eyes narrowed. With every word she uttered, it seemed she was working her way toward more and more trouble. "Actually, Sophie, no I don't know," he said, his voice deceptively pleasant. "Why don't you tell me? What do they say?"

Sophie nearly choked on her own tongue, especially with the predatory way he was watching her. She was suddenly beginning to have a lot more sympathy for the gazelles in the wildlife programs Noah liked to watch on Saturday mornings.

"You're the doctor."

"I am. What I also am is pretty skilled at figuring out when someone is snowing me."

"Snowing you? It's eighty degrees out!" She was playing dumb, but as soon as the words left her mouth she knew that she'd gone too far. Sure enough, Jack pushed his chair back from the table and stalked slowly toward her, a twisted little smile on his lips that was somewhere between a grin and a smirk.

"Maybe, but it's about twenty degrees below zero in here."

That shut her up. Was he saying she was cold and making him feel unwelcome? She puzzled over it a few seconds, but then it was too late because Jack was towering over her, his wonderful amber eyes filled with a mixture of amusement and disdain.

"You aren't actually trying to tell me that that's your whole reaction to this afternoon, are you? The whole, 'it was nice but not a big deal'? I know you're not that kind of woman, Sophie."

"What kind of woman is that?" she asked, vaguely offended. She wasn't a prude.

"The kind who blows a guy off after sex."

Is that what he thought she was doing? She licked her lips nervously, swallowed convulsively. Tried to take a step back, but he had her completely trapped. The center island was at her back, Jack—stormy-eyed and sarcastic—was in front of her, and his arms were on either side of her.

"I was trying to say that I had a really good time," the words came out with difficulty. She seemed to suddenly be a little breathless. She could feel him pressed against her and it was quite obvious that he was aroused. Maybe she'd jumped the gun on when she assumed he came over to let her down easy. "I didn't want you to think I expect anything from you."

"I spent over two hours this afternoon getting to know your body as intimately as is possible. I think you've got the right to expect something from me. Don't you?"

"A lot of men don't feel that way."

"I thought we were friends. Haven't you figured out yet that I'm not most men?" He lifted a hand to her face, stroked his fingers gently down her cheek and she had to fight to keep her eyes open. Every nerve ending she had was shimmering in plea-sure, urging her to relax and let him do again all the wicked, wonderful things he'd shown her earlier in the day.

"I'm lousy at reading signals," she admitted as she shivered despite her best efforts to stay strong.

He smiled a little at that. Brushed his thumb across her lips. Instinctively she opened up, letting him in.

His jaw tightened and the tension between them ratcheted up about a hundred knots. He turned so that his palm could cup her face and it was then that she felt the rough scratch of scar tissue. She realized he'd been touching her with his injured hand the entire time. He'd never done that before, was always too self-conscious about his injury to draw any sort of attention to it at all.

Her lust-fogged brain struggled to make sense of what it meant. Was he finally relaxed enough around her not to worry about his hand? Or was she reading too much into it? She didn't know and that was frustrating. "So you don't expect anything from me? Despite our activities earlier this afternoon?" he asked silkily. The look on his face was smoldering, nearly melting her into a puddle. Which, she realized as understanding dawned, was exactly what he was intending. The jerk.

But what was good for the goose… Lowering her voice, she gave him her version of the seductive look he was currently leveling at her. "You really have to ask?" she said in her breathiest Marilyn Monroe impression. "How many times did I scream your name today?"

He reared back a little in surprise, but after a second his pupils dilated and he pressed closer, until his lips were a breath away from her own. "I stopped counting at twenty-seven."

Her brain was so lust fogged that it took a few seconds for what he said to register. When it did, she gasped. "Twenty—"

His knowing grin confirmed everything. "You jerk! You're playing with me."

He pushed back from the counter with a smirk. "Really? I've been playing you, little miss, 'we both had a really good time…'" He used his fingers to make quotations marks around the words.

"I did have a good time," she told him.

"So did I," Jack told her. "Which is why I'm wondering when we can do it again? Sans me falling into an orgasm-induced coma, that is."

She laughed. She couldn't help herself. Though she knew there was another side to Jack, one that was dark and tormented and hurt, she had to admit that she really liked the fun, playful side of him, too. She wished that she'd known him before the injury. Then maybe she'd be able to figure out who he really was. Was the charming, carefree persona a defense to keep others from seeing inside him? Or was it who he really was, underneath all the hurt?

"I kind of liked the orgasm-induced coma," she told him, shoving her worries away, at least for the time being. "It gave me a chance to cuddle with you for a little while."

"Yes, well, cuddling's even better when both partners are awake for it," he said, pulling her into his arms to demonstrate.

And she had to admit, he was right. It felt really nice to be pressed up against his beating heart, his chin resting on her head while his arms wrapped around her waist. As the pencil sharpener stopped whirring away upstairs and little feet clomped their way down the stairs, she told him as much.

His lips skimmed across her cheek. "You smell good."

"Thank you." She sniffed him. "And so do you."

"Mom!" Noah's voice drifted in from the family room, where she could hear the TV playing the theme song to Kyle's favorite cartoon—an occasion that was sure to annoy Noah. "Are you guys coming?"

"Absolutely!" Jack called back. "Don't roll any green guys without me."

"He has a name you know," Noah shouted.

"And you can tell us all about it in a minute," she told him before reluctantly pulling her arms from around Jack's waist. "Is that what we are now?" she asked him seriously. "Partners of some sort?"

He sighed. "I don't know what we are. That whole thing that happened this afternoon was great, but it screwed everything up."

Her heart clenched a little at that, but she battled

the feeling back down. Just friends, she reminded herself. Nothing more. "I thought you said you didn't regret it?"

"I don't. Are you kidding me? But that doesn't mean I don't wish we'd done things in a more normal order. Defined the boundaries early on."

"Like?"

"Like me taking you out to dinner, wooing you a little. You're the one who gave me flowers."

"Yes, but rumor has it you gave me twenty-seven orgasms, so I think we're even."

"Okay, so it was more like nine," he said with a grin.

"Actually, it was more like eleven." She picked up a piece of pasta from his dish and popped it in her mouth. "Not that I was counting or anything. Partner."

CHAPTER TWELVE

EARLY THE NEXT morning, Jack was outside in his rapidly growing-out-of-control front yard, armed with a new pair of gardening shears and a black plastic bag, when Sophie breezed down her front walkway, Noah and Kyle at her heels. She looked beautiful and rested and serene, and it somehow managed to put him in an even grumpier mood because he was none of the three.

His shift had ended at six, and he'd come home with every intention of falling into bed. But yesterday had ruined even that for him. When he went upstairs to his room, all he could smell was Sophie. Which had aroused him, made him want her until he had no chance at sleep at all. Frustration had sent him out here to do something about the yard, but fifteen minutes of fighting his landscaping—and losing—had his patience wearing thin.

"Hey, Jack!" Kyle called.

Gritting his teeth, he fought back his irritation and sent the kid the most genuine smile he could manage. "Hey, Yahtzee King. Where you going?"

"To the lake! We're going to rent some kayaks

and go rowing. Plus Mom brought some bread to feed the ducks."

"Wow. That sounds like fun."

"It is!"

"Well, have a good time. And feed some ducks for me, will you?"

"You could come with us, if you'd like," Sophie said as she headed over to him. "Feed the ducks yourself."

He dropped the shears into the bushes before she got too close. Call it ego, call it pride, but whatever it was, he didn't want the woman he was currently sleeping with to see how much he was struggling with the shears. It was a stupid gardening task, something Kyle could do without much difficulty, and he was barely able to manage it. With his left hand, which was more than strong enough to work the shears, he had almost no control, so he kept snipping off the wrong branches, while his right hand didn't even have enough strength to get the blades open let alone closed again when a branch was between the blades.

He should have simply hired a gardener as he'd originally intended, but his physical therapist had suggested the shears as a way to strengthen his hand, get more mobility back, both of which he desperately wanted. But it turned out what was a great suggestion in theory, left him totally screwed in practice.

"What are you doing out here, anyway?" Sophie asked, curious.

"Just checking everything out. Seeing what needs to be done."

"Oh." She nodded at the shrub he was currently standing in the middle of. "That needs to be cut back before it gets cold. Otherwise, it'll die."

No shit, Sherlock. That's why I'm out here making a damn fool of myself. The retort came automatically, but he bit it back. No use hurting Sophie's feelings just because he was in a bear of a mood.

"I'll make a note of that," he finally answered, teeth clenched into a smile that felt—and probably looked—more like a grimace of pain.

"I have the name of a good gardener. Maybe you could call him? He's the brother of one of my clients and—" She broke off abruptly. "Is something wrong? You look…" She was quiet for a few seconds, searching for the right word, but finally settled on, "You look savage."

He felt savage. And stupid. And so many other things he didn't even know where to start. But most of all, he felt crippled. He hated every second of it. Shoving his good hand through his hair in frustration, he made an effort to smooth out his face. To smile. It took a second, but he managed it. "I'm fine."

"Yeah, I can tell." For a minute he thought she was going to say something else, but then she just looked at him. "So, do you want to go?"

"Go where?"

She nodded toward the boys. "To the lake with us. To feed the ducks." When he didn't respond, she asked, "Is any of this sounding familiar to you at all?"

"Oh, right. Of course." He shook his head. "I can't go."

"Big plans?" she teased with an arch of an eyebrow.

"Something like that." Drowning himself in self-pity. That counted as big plans, didn't it?

"Well, have fun. And good look with the yard. I guess I'll see you tonight?"

He nodded. "Seven o'clock."

"You want me to meet you at your house? That way—"

"I'm not so crippled I can't pick my date up at the door, you know."

Sophie reared back in surprise, her eyes darkening with an empathy he couldn't stand to see. He didn't want empathy, any more than he wanted sympathy or pity or any of the other emotions people seemed to feel when they looked at him these days. He wanted to go back to being Dr. Jack Alexander, trauma surgeon and clinic supervisor. But these days, that guy seemed a long way off.

"I didn't mean—"

"I know exactly what you meant." He kept pushing at her, acting like a total jerk. But he couldn't help himself. He'd put up with that look from Amanda. From Simon. From his family and coworkers and friends. He'd even put up with the look from his patients. But he would be damned if he would put up with it from his lover. "Yes, I was shot. But that didn't make me less of a man. I thought I proved that to you yesterday."

She blanched, pressed her lips tightly together as they stood there, staring at each other.

Finally, when it became apparent that he wasn't going to say anything else, she said, "I don't think I'm the one you need to prove that to. I only suggested meeting you at your house because your car is parked over here. But by all means, feel free to drive thirty feet to pick me up." She paused to look him over from head to toe, the glint in her eye saying clearly that she found him lacking. "I'll be waiting with bated breath."

Then she spun and headed back to Kyle and Noah, who were waiting for them with wide eyes and happy grins. He watched their shoulders slump a little when she told them he wasn't coming and ushered them toward her SUV, watched as she got Kyle strapped into his booster seat and a picnic basket stowed in the trunk.

The indignant swish of her hips as she walked around to the driver's side door made him feel like even more of an ass than he already did. Which was exactly what she'd intended. And exactly what he'd deserved.

SOPHIE WAS PISSED. There was no other word for it. Not angry. Not annoyed. Completely and royally pissed. She didn't know what the hell kind of bug had crawled up Jack's spine between last night's Yahtzee game and this morning's sidewalk debacle, but something clearly had.

Which was fine. He was entitled to his moods. He was a doctor, after all. He saw a lot of rough things on a pretty regular basis. Plus, he was probably tired from his shift in the clinic as it was too early for him to have slept much. Not to mention the fact that it had been obvious he was in pain from the way he kept flexing his hand and shifting his weight onto his good leg.

Any of those reasons alone gave him the right to be a little short, a little antagonistic. She understood that. In the months after Jeff had died, she hadn't exactly been at her best. But Jack had gone way beyond grumpy. He had been downright rude when she had done nothing to deserve it. That was what she really didn't appreciate.

What had she ever done to make him think his injuries were an issue for her? He claimed he'd proved his manhood in bed with her the night before. She barely stifled a snort at the absurdity of his accusation. Hadn't she proven that she enjoyed being with him, enjoyed knowing him, bum hand or not? She really didn't think she could have been any more responsive had she tried.

Ugh. She slammed her hands against the steering wheel in frustration. Why did men have to be so egotistical and annoying? For God's sake, she'd offered to walk to his house, not trim the damn bushes for him. Though she knew very well that was what he'd been out there trying to do. She'd seen him struggling with the hedge clipper from her living-room window, long before she'd ever set foot outside.

The way he thought about himself drove her absolutely nuts. With everyone else, Jack was a bottomless well of compassion and patience and understanding. She'd seen him with her boys, listened more than once in the past couple of weeks as he called patients to follow up with them when any normal doctor would be asleep. He answered their questions with no hint of impatience or annoyance, yet he expected so much more from himself. He wouldn't stand for any weakness on his own part, even though it was obvious he'd been through the wringer and that he was still trying to work a lot of stuff out. Which was fine with her. Really. But he didn't need to be such a jerk about it.

Swinging the car into a parking spot, she helped her boys out and then headed down the path that led to the lake, determined to snap out of the bad mood Jack had put her in. She and the boys hadn't done a fun outing in weeks and she was determined to relax and focus on them instead of Jack and the chaos he'd added to her already-full life.

"Mom, Mom!" Noah called as he ran a little ahead of her. "Can we get the blue kayak?"

"Is it a three-seater?"

"No, only two." He grinned angelically. "But we

don't really need three seats. Kyle can swim next to the boat, can't you, Kyle?"

Her youngest son turned white. "But I'm only learning how to swim! I can't swim that far."

"Sure you can. It'll be good practice for you. Don't be a scaredy-cat."

"I'm not! If you're so brave, why don't you swim?"

"I already have. Duh. When I was five, Mom tossed me out of the boat and left me to swim or drown. You'd better be careful because she'll probably do it to you. Maybe even today."

As Kyle's lower lip started to quiver, Sophie stepped in, praying for patience as she did. "Knock it off, Noah! No one's going swimming."

Kyle ran up to her and burrowed into her side, his little arm wrapped around her waist. "Promise, Mommy? You won't toss me in?"

Sighing in exasperation, she shot Noah a look that told him to knock it off. His only response was an even more innocent grin. The little stinker. What was it about older brothers that made them feel like they had the right to torture their younger siblings? One would think that resentment at being usurped as the only child would only last so long, but it seemed that they could carry a grudge for years. Or at least Noah could. It drove her nuts.

Squatting down so that she was eye to eye with Kyle, she wrapped him in a big hug and told him, "I promise not to toss you in. I don't, however, make the same promise about Noah."

Noah laughed like a hyena, completely secure in the fact that she would never do any such thing. But Kyle, despite everything, defended his brother. "Don't do that, Mommy. Noah could drownded."

"Are you sure? Isn't it a good punishment for him being mean to you?"

"No, Mommy! I love Noah. Don't make him drownded."

She narrowed her eyes, pretended reluctance. "Well, if you insist…"

"I do, I do!"

"Okay, then. Let's go get the big yellow kayak." She pointed ahead of them. "It looks like a three-seater."

"But I don't like yellow!" Noah started to whine. But when she shot him a you're-on-thin-ice glare, he shut up pretty quickly.

The rest of the morning went pretty smoothly. Within ten minutes she had rented a kayak and started the fun, but slightly arduous, task of rowing them from one end of the lake to the other. The boys tried to help, but the truth was they were often more hindrance than help. Which was fine. She hadn't brought them out here to win a race, after all.

No, she thought, as she fell into a rhythm guaranteed to leave her with sore shoulders in the morning, she came out here with the boys because she loved being with them without the distraction of TV and video games. Loved listening to them as they chattered about school and superheroes and their favorite movies. What she had with them was so different than what she had with her own mother—or with any of her foster moms—that she wanted to grab on to it with both hands and never let go.

Which was a problem, she admitted, because she had a tendency to want to hold on too tightly. She loved Noah and Kyle, loved them with a fierceness she never would have imagined possible nine years ago. She loved their smiles and their sweetness, their penchant for mischief and their indomitable spirits. Honestly, she loved everything about them.

Some days she stood at their doors and watched them sleep, overwhelmed by the knowledge that these beautiful, amazing creatures were hers. The first people in the world she'd ever truly loved. The first people in the world to ever truly love her.

They came first with her and always would. Their happiness and health and security was more important to her than anything else on earth. She knew part of her desire to do everything right with them, to be there for every scratched knee and every personal triumph stemmed from the fact that growing up, she had never had that. She'd never had parents who put aside their own issues or desires in order to help her with hers, never had anyone she could turn to who she knew would be there unconditionally. Just like she'd never had anyone that she knew would put her first.

Oh, Jeff had cared about her. She knew that. And she had loved him in her own way. But even he, her husband, never put her first. What he wanted was always more important than anything she wanted. What Jeff's dead father had wanted. What the army wanted. To be honest, that had been fine with her—partly because she hadn't known any better and partly because she'd never loved Jeff, not the way a wife should love her husband. She'd worked hard to be the kind of wife Jeff wanted. She'd built a life with him, a good life, because she'd wanted a family. Children. Someone she really could love unconditionally.

She thanked God every day for giving her Noah and Kyle. Even, she acknowledged ruefully, on the days when they seemed determined to drive her out of her mind. Days like today.

"Stop splashing me with your paddle, you dork!" Noah growled at Kyle.

"I'm not doing it on purpose! I'm just rowing."

"Yeah, well, you're rowing all over me. Stop it!"

"Guys, come on," she told them. "This is supposed to be fun."

"Tell him that!" Noah complained. "He's getting my shirt all wet—"

"No, I'm not!" an aggrieved Kyle shouted. "I'm just rowing." Of course, he chose that moment to smack his paddle into the water for emphasis and water sprayed in both directions, hitting her on the chest and Noah straight in the eyes!

"You jerk!" Noah spluttered, trying to find a dry spot on his shirt to wipe his eyes. "That burns."

"I didn't mean to," Kyle said in his sad little brother voice, but she'd been around the block enough to see the gleam of unholy joy dancing right underneath the fake remorse.

"Kyle Anthony Connors, you need to apologize to—"

She broke off as Noah, who had obviously seen the glee as well, stuck his paddle in the water and sent a huge oar full of water straight into Kyle's face.

That was all it took. Before she could even open her mouth, World Water War Twenty-Eight was off and running as the boys started splashing each other as rapidly as they could. Though she was at the end, she still caught quite a bit of the action, in those first few seconds as the kayak tipped and shuddered beneath them.

"Hey!" she finally managed to get out. "Knock it off."

The boys were too busy trying to kill each other to notice. She grabbed Kyle by the shoulder and pulled him back so that his ear was at her mouth. "I said that's enough." She trotted out the mom voice she reserved for only truly awful transgressions.

He settled down pretty quickly, but Noah kept it up until she swung her paddle up and smacked him lightly on the arm to get his attention.

"Ow!" he howled, though she'd barely tapped him.

"Keep it up and we're going home. No ducks, no picnic, nothing. Do I make myself clear?"

"He splashed me first!"

"And you splashed him last. Looks pretty even to me." She sighed impatiently. "Now, you've got two choices and ten seconds to make the decision. Continue splashing each other and we'll go home. Or get along and we can stay for a while. At this point, I don't actually care which it is. But make your decision now." She glanced at her watch to show that she was counting the seconds down.

"Stay!" Kyle shouted. "Please, Mommy!"

"Stay," Noah said, much more grudgingly.

"Fine. No more splashing because I have no desire to swim back to shore and I know neither of you do, either." She rummaged in the bag at her feet, tossed each boy a bag of bread as a distraction. "Now why don't you get busy feeding the ducks while I row?"

Which, thank God, was exactly what they did.

The next three hours passed in blissful harmony, broken only by the occasional, easily squashed squabble. But as they were heading back to the car, Noah asked, "Are you going to marry Dr. Jack?"

The question surprised her so much that she stumbled, and dropped the picnic basket. The remains of their lunch spilled on the ground, but she barely noticed as she tried to figure out where on earth that question had come from. Nothing came to mind.

"Mommy, you made a mess!" Kyle giggled, dropping to his knees next to the basket to start picking up the mess.

"I sure did," she agreed, squatting to help him.

Noah didn't move, however, but stared at her with wary eyes as he waited for an answer.

She waited to talk to him until they were back at the car and Kyle was once again strapped into his booster seat.

"Honey," she asked Noah, "Why would you think Jack and I were going to get married?"

"So, you're not?"

"No, sweetheart. We're just friends. He's helping me out by babysitting you guys and I pay him back with dinner sometimes. That's it."

Noah didn't answer her, staring back at her with serious brown eyes, so like his father that she had to force herself not to look away. Especially when she remembered exactly what she and Jack had been up to the day before.

Finally, when she was about to give up waiting, he whispered, "I saw you."

Her heart went crazy, even as she told herself it was impossible. That he'd been at school the whole time she was in bed with Jack. "Saw me doing what?"

"Kissing Dr. Jack. In the kitchen last night, before the Yahtzee game."

When she thought he'd been safely ensconced in the family room, watching cartoons. He must have come looking for them.

She felt her cheeks heat up as she tried to figure out what to do, what to say. Noah had been three when his father had shipped out to Afghanistan, so his memories of him were murky at best. She did what she could to talk about him regularly, to tell stories that would help the boys get a feeling for who their father had been.

She didn't know how much it helped—certainly not as much as having a real, live dad to play baseball with—but she'd done her best. Now, as she studied Noah's stoic little face for some kind of clue as to what he was thinking or feeling, she wondered what she was supposed to say. There hadn't been a man in her life since Jeff, and while Jack wasn't exactly *in her life,* he was the closest thing the boys had ever had to a male influence. The closest thing she'd ever had to a lover, even though they hadn't defined their relationship as such.

Since no clues were forthcoming, and she'd been totally blindsided by Noah's question, Sophie finally decided to go for the truth. Or at least as much of the truth as her eight-year-old son could handle. "Jack and I are friends," she told him. "We like each other very much and sometimes when adult's like each other, they kiss."

He rolled his eyes at her. "I'm not a baby, Mom. I've seen grown-ups kiss on TV lots of times."

"Oh, right. Well, then, Jack and I are kind of like that. Friends who kiss, but who both care about you and Kyle an awful lot." She bent so they were on the same eye level. It didn't take much, as her son had grown so much recently that he was only a few inches shorter than she was. It was a bittersweet realization, one that she didn't have time to reflect on right now but that she would probably cry a little bit over later.

"But if this bothers you, me kissing Jack, you need to tell me so we can talk about it. You know there's no one in the world I love more than you and Kyle." Not that she was necessarily going to stop, because, wow, the man was truly gifted—injured hand or not.

"I know, Mom. I thought, maybe it'd be cool if Dr. Jack moved in. You know, kind of like Kyle and I would have a dad like the other boys in my class."

Oh, boy. Sophie blew out a huge breath, trying to buy some time. She really hadn't seen that coming, had thought the boys were completely satisfied with their single-parent home. Obviously, though, she'd been wrong.

It stung a little, deep inside that she alone wasn't enough for her sons. But she shoved it back down, because, one, this wasn't about her and two, of course Noah was looking for a father figure. He was an eight-year-old boy. And though she'd learned to field a baseball with the best of them, she still wasn't dad material. And—despite his moods and the darkness he couldn't seem to get out from under—Jack really was dad material.

"Oh, Noah," she said, pulling him into her arms. "Jack isn't going to be your new dad. He's going to leave in a few months and then we'll probably never see him again."

"Why does he have to go?" There were enough

tears in Noah's voice—though none spilled onto his cheeks—to turn the sting into something more painful. "I'll miss him, Mom."

"I know, baby. So will I. But Dr. Jack has a super-important job. He takes care of little boys and girls who don't have anyone else to take care of them. They don't have hospitals or pediatricians or any of the things we do, so he goes there so that they can get the medicine and the operations that they need."

Noah considered her words for a minute or so, then nodded. "I guess that's more important than babysitting us."

"Not more important, sweetheart, more urgent. There are kids who would die if Dr. Jack didn't help them."

"I get it now." He climbed into the car, fastened his seat belt. Then looked at her through the still-open door. "I wish you could be with someone who didn't always have to leave." He pulled out his MP3 player and stuck the earbuds in his ears.

The conversation had ended easily—she'd obviously given the right answers. But as Sophie walked around to the driver's seat, instead of feeling like she'd dodged a bullet, all she felt was sad. Because Noah wasn't the only one who wished the men she ended up caring about were also men who could stick around for a while. Other women had no problem finding men who were home every night by six. What did the fact that she couldn't say about her?

CHAPTER THIRTEEN

JACK DRESSED FOR dinner with mixed feelings. He had originally dreaded this dinner—the idea of watching Amanda and Simon make goo-goo eyes at each other all night left him cold, no matter how happy he was that their lives were moving forward so beautifully. But in the past couple days, his attitude had changed.

Once Sophie had said she'd go with him, he'd started looking forward to it. Seeing her dressed up, spending time with her at a nice restaurant, introducing her to his friends, all seemed like a really great idea. She was a beautiful, kind, happy woman, one who made him laugh in a way no one had in a very long time, if ever. Not to mention she was incredible in bed. He'd spent quite a bit of time the past twenty-four hours reliving what it had been like to make love to her and imagining all the things he was going to do to her once he got her back in his bed.

But now she was probably angry with him. She'd come over this morning to invite him to do something with her and the boys—something he would probably have enjoyed very much—and he'd jumped down her throat because of his own insecurities. He'd been rude and accusatory and there'd been no call for it. Which meant his chance of getting her back in his bed this evening were slim to none.

It also meant that he was going to have to apologize for being such an ass. Again, nothing more than he deserved, but he dreaded—absolutely dreaded—the explanation that would have to go along with the apology. The last thing he wanted to do was draw attention to all the things he couldn't do because of his injury, but any explanation of his churlish behavior would have to include that.

He'd been trying to work up a speech in his head all afternoon, one that didn't make him look like a total loser. So far he hadn't come up with anything. After all, no woman wanted a man who was drowning in self-pity.

After checking his tie for a second time, and wondering if he would end up wanting to hang himself with it by the end of the night, Jack slipped his wallet and keys into his pocket and drove over to collect Sophie. Which reinforced what an ass he'd been when she'd suggested meeting him at his house. It was ridiculous to move the car from his driveway to hers, and if he'd been less of a pathetic asshole earlier, he would have seen that she was trying to make things as logistical and easy as possible.

It was a wonder she was still interested in going out with him at all.

Pasting a smile on his face that he was far from feeling, Jack rang the doorbell, impatient for Sophie to answer. The sooner he could get the apology portion of the evening over and move onto other things, the better.

He'd be as honest as he could be. Tell her he'd been having a really rough morning and apologize for being churlish. Sophie didn't strike him as the kind of woman to insist being given a pound of flesh to prove his sincerity, so maybe... Sophie opened her door and anything he'd been planning to say flew right out of his head as every drop of blood in his brain travelled three feet south of his head.

The first thought that entered his lust-frozen brain was that he'd been wrong when he'd figured Sophie would wear a suit. Way wrong. His second thought was that she should wear dresses more often because she looked stunning. Absolutely gorgeous. Tonight, there was nothing of the mom or the lawyer to be found in her.

Instead, she was all redheaded sex goddess. Dressed in a green and gold wraparound dress that hugged the lush, round landscape of her breasts and hips like a second skin. His hands wanted to run over her beautiful curves. The plunging neckline didn't help matters, as it showcased her high, beautiful breasts—reminding him of how much he'd enjoyed licking his way over them the day before. The knee-length hemline showcased her long legs, legs that were shown off to their best advantage by a pair of very high, very sexy, gold-stiletto heels.

For long seconds he did nothing but stare at her,

mouth dry and vocal cords frozen as he remembered the way those legs had wrapped around his waist when they'd made love.

"Is something wrong?" she finally asked with a nervous little laugh. He glanced up in time to see her tuck a strand of her beautiful red hair behind her ear.

"No, of course not. I'm blown away by how beautiful you look tonight." He held out the flowers he'd picked up for her. They were just daisies, nothing special, but when he'd seen them he'd thought of Sophie's sunny smile and hadn't been able to resist them. Now, though, as she blushed a little, glanced away, he couldn't help wondering if he'd screwed up again. Maybe he should have gone with the roses, even though they'd seemed so normal and predictable, something their relationship definitely wasn't.

"Thanks," she told him, slipping the flowers into her arms. "Let me get these some water." As she walked away, she buried her face in the flowers and he felt everything inside him relax. She did like them, after all.

She was only gone a minute or so, and when she returned, Noah and Kyle were both standing in the hall, looking at her with interest. For once, Noah's expression was quiet, contemplative. But Kyle looked totally disgusted and his little nose wrinkled as he watched her cross the foyer back to Jack.

"Ew, gross! You look like a girl, Mom."

That broke the ice, had both of them laughing as she introduced Jack to her babysitter for the night and then kissed the boys goodnight. "Be good for Sabrina," she told them. "And straight to bed after the movie is over."

"What movie?" Kyle asked, bouncing around like a kangaroo.

"The one I rented for you," Sophie said. "Which you will not get to see until all the veggies are gone from your plates."

"But, Sabrina says—"

"Sabrina knows she answers to me," Sophie told him with a wink at the woman. "No buts and no complaints." Leaning down, she kissed the top of his head again, then linked arms with Jack and pulled him out the door. "If we don't get going now, we never will. They're masters of the long good-bye."

He escorted her to the car, wondering as he did how often she went on dates. The boys had taken her imminent departure in stride, and they seemed to have a routine down with Sabrina, as well. Not that it was any of his business or anything. It wasn't like they had any kind of commitment between them, but still. He was curious because…well, because.

"I'm really sorry about this morning," he told her, biting the bullet as he held the car door open for her.

She eyed him for a second, her beautiful green eyes shadowed despite the streetlight directly above them. Then she inclined her head, smiled. "Everyone has a bad day occasionally. Let's forget about it."

That was it? No recriminations? No groveling necessary? Somehow her easy dismissal made him feel about a million times worse. All he said, though, was "Thanks. It won't happen again."

Sophie nodded.

"We're meeting Simon and Amanda at Eugene's," he told her once he'd pulled out of the driveway. "I haven't been, but they say it's delicious."

"It is. Not to mention a culinary adventure—the menu is always changing, and always a little different than anything else around. They have really strange ideas sometimes, but somehow they always end up being delicious."

"Well, then I'm looking forward to the evening."

"Me, too." She smiled at him, and her beautifully painted mouth had him imaging the things she might do with it later.

"The light's green," she told him as a car behind him honked. He sped through the intersection, wondering what had gotten into him. Yes, they'd had mind-blowing sex. And, yes, he wanted to do it again as soon as possible. But that didn't mean he couldn't behave like a civilized person for the length of one dinner date. Still, he couldn't resist another quick glance at her out of the corner of his eye. She looked like every fantasy he'd ever had rolled into one.

They talked about work the rest of the way to the restaurant. He was glad to have a few amusing stories from the clinic that week, instead of the usual stories of poverty, pain, and desperation. Then he asked her how the court case she'd been working on had gone.

"Really well, actually. We got everything we asked for, so it couldn't have gone better."

"You know, I don't think I even know what kind of law you practice."

She glanced at him from under her lashes, her expression more mischievous than he had ever seen it. "What kind do you think I practice?"

"Seriously? You're going to make me guess?" he asked, but when she nodded he decided it couldn't hurt to play along. "Okay. I'll bite. So, I know you go to court pretty regularly because of your schedule and because you knew the judges well enough to know which ones are going to keep you late and which ones aren't."

She nodded. "Go on."

"You wear suits every day, even when you don't have to go to court, though you have a tendency to wear pantsuits on days when you're in the office. I'm not sure that the differentiation means anything—"

"Comfort."

"Right. Of course. But both are professional, fancy even, so that could mean big law firm or corporate." She didn't say anything, so he continued, "You don't travel a lot, or at least I don't think you do—" He looked at her for confirmation.

"Nope."

"And you keep fairly regular hours, though I have seen you go out at odd times occasionally, always dressed in a suit." He looked at her again, to check how he was doing, and he found her grinning, like she was enjoying his analysis. If he was totally honest, so was he. He hadn't realized he'd noticed so many things about her in the past few weeks, hadn't thought he was keeping track. But he supposed his subconscious had been intrigued by her long before he'd acted on it by rushing her into his bed.

"So," she asked, after he'd been quiet for a while. "Have you figured it out yet?"

"Well, I've got it narrowed down to private defense, corporate tax, or family law. At a solid firm with a good, solid reputation, but not one of the big four here in Atlanta. You just don't strike me as the kind of woman who will crawl over people's dead bodies to advance her career—which is what, I hear, a lot of attorneys at top firms have to do."

"So make a decision already. We're almost to Eugene's."

"Hmm, a little bit touchy about that last part of the analysis. That must mean I'm close." He narrowed his eyes, thought about it a little more. "Well, you don't really seem the type for corporate tax laws—"

"Thank God!"

He smiled, happy that his instincts were so right on. "And you seem a little soft for a defense attorney, so I'm going to go with family law."

"I'm not soft," she objected.

He laughed. "Yeah, right. You're a marshmallow. It's written all over your face."

"No, it's not." The words sounded deadly serious, like she was suddenly sick of the game, and when he looked at her she had wrapped her arms around herself. A second layer of protection, but he didn't know from what. He started to push, but she was much better at deflecting than he was. Not a big surprise. She was a lawyer.

"Okay. Sorry. I didn't mean to offend you." He held his hands up in the universal gesture of surrender. "You're as tough as a nail. Tougher, even. Is that hard enough for you?"

"That'll do." She forced a smile, but he could tell she didn't mean it. She was showing way more teeth than she usually did. "And I'm not offended. I hate being taken for a cream puff because I'm small and..." She broke off, gestured to the curves he hadn't been able to keep his eyes off all evening.

"I'm sorry," Jack said, slowing to a stop for a light. "I didn't realize it was a sore subject." When she didn't answer, he reached over and tipped her chin up so that she had to meet his eyes.

She sighed. "When I was in the system a lot of men tried to take advantage of me because of the way I looked, so— It's my turn to apologize. I overreacted to a conversation that I initiated. Which is stupid."

Anger welled up inside him. He'd worked in a lot of different countries through the years, countries where the light veneer of civilization had worn away years before he'd gotten there. While there, he'd seen what the strong did to the weak, what the monsters did to the innocent, simply because they could. The idea that Sophie had been subjected to something like that made him furious…and sick.

His first instinct was to press, to find out specifics of what had put that bruised look in her eyes. But this wasn't the time or the place, no matter how much he wished it was. Plus, he had his own secrets. Pushing Sophie for hers would be hypocritical in the extreme. Besides, he couldn't stand the idea of hurting her just to satisfy the vicious curiosity burning inside of him.

Still, it took a couple minutes for him to tamp the rage down, and the silence between them grew awkward, which he couldn't stand. So, determined to scale the wall that had sprung up between them before it got even higher, he did the only thing he could think of. He reverted to the beginning of the conversation. "So if you aren't a defense attorney and you aren't a tax attorney, that leaves family law. Am I right?"

He glanced at her out of the corner of his eye, watched as she did her best to shake the last vestiges of weirdness between them off. It was one of the things he really liked about her—the way she didn't hold a grudge but dove right in to help. "You're almost right. I'm the attorney of record for three battered women's shelters. I help women get divorces, obtain protection orders, file charges when applicable. The case I've been dealing with for the past two weeks was a rough one. The husband's a cop and a real bastard.

"He beat her constantly when she was with him, and when she finally worked up the nerve to leave him then he stalked her and tried to kill her. His conduct was always ignored or brushed under the carpet because of the blue line, and she couldn't get any help. By the time she came to us, she had resigned herself to the idea that she was going to die. All she cared about was making sure her children were safe."

Her fists clenched in her lap, her nails digging into her palms for long seconds before she relaxed again.

"You helped her?" he asked.

"We were able to push the divorce through yesterday and get a restraining order. Plus her husband's lieutenant was ordered by the judge to deliver a departmental reprimand that goes on his record and could affect his pension if there are more incidences, so basically it was a slam dunk in all areas. Thank God."

"You did all that?"

"Marlena helped. She was so unshakable on the stand, so calm and determined. I'm so proud of her and how far she's come in such a short time."

"How long have you been working with her?" he asked as he pulled into the restaurant parking lot.

"Four and a half months."

He stared at her, amazed. "That's incredible. You're incredible. I had no idea that's what you were doing."

"You thought I was charging five hundred dol-

lars an hour in some swanky office building somewhere, huh?"

"I guess I did." He reached forward, brushed away
a lock of hair that had fallen in front of her face. It
wrapped around his finger, a silky flame that chased
away a little bit of the cold that had taken up resi-
dence inside him. "Seriously, I'm really impressed."

"It's really not that impressive. More paperwork
than anything else. It's a far cry from, oh, I don't
know, running off to disaster-stricken nations to
bring medical care to people who rarely have electricity or running water. I still have indoor plumbing
and air-conditioning, so you totally kick my butt in
the whole contest."

"Well, there is that. Indoor plumbing and central
air cannot be underappreciated."

"That's what I'm saying."

He pulled into a parking spot and turned off the
car. "Still, you done good, kid." He winked at her
and she smiled, a shy little upturning of her lips that
said, clearer than words, that Sophie wasn't used to
getting compliments. Leaning forward, he pressed
a soft kiss to her forehead. Another one to her left
cheek and a third to her right. She shuddered a little,
her hands sliding over his chest, tangling in his shirt
as she tilted her face up to his.

She looked beautiful. Her green eyes luminous in
the moonlight, her long, red hair glowing with sil-
vered flames. Her sweet pink lips parted a little bit
as he ran his thumb over their softness.

She gasped then a little, and he took the opportunity to slide his thumb against the edge of her teeth.

Sophie tensed, opened more, then sucked the pad of his thumb inside the warm heat of her mouth, biting down with her sharp, little teeth. It took every ounce of control he had not to lift her up and over the center console, onto his lap, steering wheel or not.

Figuring that would embarrass her, but needing more—so much more—than she was currently giving him, he pulled his thumb away, trailing it over her chin and down her slender, elegant neck to the pulse beating frantically at the hollow of her throat. And then, when her breath was coming faster and her eyes were glazing over, he kissed her.

JACK'S MOUTH on hers nearly made Sophie scream at the heat of it. The sexiness of it. The downright deliciousness of it.

He tasted like he smelled—of sex and satin sheets and long, sultry nights.

He was delicious, and she wanted more, so much more than the meeting of their mouths could give her.

Her hands crept up his neck to bury themselves in his shaggy hair. It was cool and silky against her fingers and felt so good she couldn't help grabbing on. Tugging a little, so that his lips were pressed even more firmly against her own. And then she surrendered completely, giving herself over to the heat flashing between them.

She'd thought maybe she'd exaggerated the heat of

yesterday afternoon, blown up the encounter in her own mind until she remembered it as hotter than it had actually been. After all, the first time a woman made love in five years was bound to be intense.

But she'd been wrong. This moment, this kiss, was as wicked and wild and wonderful as she remembered. Maybe even more so, since they'd had all those hours yesterday to learn each other. Whatever was on offer, she was going to take it. Take him.

Jack's lips were hard against her own, firm but a little out of control. And his tongue—it was everywhere. It swept over her bottom lip, nuzzled at the corner of her mouth before darting inside and stroking against her own tongue. Back and forth, over the roof of her mouth, down her cheek, along the inside of her upper lip before delving deep to explore the most hidden recesses of her.

She gasped, and he pulled back a little, a questioning look in his eyes. But she refused to let him go—not yet, not now when she had barely gotten a taste of him. Instead, she pressed her advantage and sucked his lower lip between her teeth.

He groaned, and the hand at the small of her back slipped lower to cup and knead her bottom. It was her turn to moan, and as she did, he hit a button that moved his seat back. Before she knew what was happening, he had lifted her over onto his lap. Her tailbone rested against the steering wheel, her legs straddled his and her sex was nestled against his hardness.

She saw stars—there was no other word for the blinding flashes of light that pulsed behind her closed eyelids—and her hands slipped down to clutch at his neck, his shoulders, his chest.

A warning bell was going off in the back of her head, telling her this wasn't the time or the place for this. But she couldn't bring herself to care. Not now, when his lips were skimming over her neck and his hands were anchored on her hips, lifting and lowering her against him.

Heat moved inside of her with every flex of his hips, building and building and building until all she could see or feel or think was him. She moaned, pressed closer, needing a little bit more stimulation.

Jack seemed to understand, because his good hand came between them, slipped into the open neckline of her dress, and cupped her breast. His thumb brushed back and forth against her nipple, once, twice, again and again until she was in a fever pitch of excitement. Then he squeezed, lightly, and she exploded, gasping his name as fireworks went off deep inside her.

Jack held her for long seconds, stroking his hands over the sensitive skin at the nape of her neck as she tried to get her breath back.

Reality crept in slowly and when it did, she felt her cheeks start to burn. She'd let Jack bring her to orgasm in a restaurant parking lot, while his friends waited inside. Even worse, she'd taken everything he'd offered and given nothing in return. She could still feel him resting, hot and hard, against her sex.

Too embarrassed to look at him, she buried her face in his neck. Moaned. "I'm so sorry.

"I'm not." He shifted a little, and as he did he pressed more deeply against her. It was his turn to groan.

"Do you want me to…" Her voice drifted away because she was too embarrassed to say out loud what she was offering. But she slid her hand down his chest to his belt buckle, in case he misunderstood what she was offering.

Jack laughed, even as he caught her hand in his, pressing a kiss to the center of her palm. "Much as I'd love to take you up on that offer, we're already late." He lifted her gingerly off his lap, returning her to her side of the car. "But when we're done in there, I will definitely take you up on your offer."

As he got out of the car, adjusting himself, she flipped the sun visor down and checked out her appearance in the mirror. He circled the car, opened her door for her and she moaned as she combed frantic fingers through her hair. "Oh my God, I look like I had sex in a car."

"You did have sex in a car—or close enough," he told her, holding a hand out to help her out. She stood facing him, and he straightened her dress for her, his hand lingering over her neckline.

She swatted him away. "I thought you said we were late?"

"Yeah, well, one more minute won't hurt." He pulled her toward him and, this time, kissed her gently on the lips.

Then he cleared his throat, asked, "So, are you ready?"

Something in his tone sounded a little off. "You make it sound like we're going to the guillotine."

"Not at all. Amanda and Simon are great."

"But?"

"But nothing." He held out an arm to her, waited for her to take it. "You'll love them," he told her confidently. Too bad the look in his eyes told a different story. Suddenly she was uneasy on a whole new level, one that had nothing to do with the fact that her dress was wrinkled and her lipstick long gone.

CHAPTER FOURTEEN

JACK'S FRIENDS WERE waiting for them in the bar, but
when he led her toward them, Sophie froze. "You
didn't tell me your friend Simon was Simon Hart!"
she whispered furiously. She'd been a fan of the
journalist and his heavy-hitting, investigative doc-
umentaries for years and had been thrilled when he'd
moved to CNN, where she could watch him regularly.

"I didn't realize it mattered," he told her, bemused.
"Are you a fan?"

"You could say that."

"Great. We should all get along really well, then."

He put a firm hand on her lower back and guided
her toward the table. But the closer they got, the more
nervous she became. Simon had been her idol since
she'd seen a story he did on Bosnia in the late nine-
ties. He'd dug deeper than a lot of people had at the
time and had been one of the first Western journal-
ists to report on the atrocities that had happened to
women and children of all the races in the shadow
of the ethnic cleansings.

She'd been in her last year of high school and toying with the idea of becoming a journalist. While she'd eventually decided to go to law school instead, she'd had a crush on Simon until she was well into her twenties. It was ridiculous, but there it was.

She started to tell Jack as much, figuring they could have a good laugh over it, but the first solid look she got at his face told her this wasn't a good time. It also told her that though hers was the back his arm was pressed against, his mind was somewhere else entirely. Namely across the bar with Amanda.

She glanced in his eyes, tried to figure out what he was thinking, then wished she hadn't, as what she saw there made her feel like a Class-A fool. He might be sleeping with her, he might even bring her flowers, but this wasn't a date. Not like she'd imagined it would be. Because where she'd once had a harmless crush on Simon Hart, Jack obviously had much more than that on Amanda.

Oh, he was subtle about it, and if she hadn't been watching him so carefully—trying to figure out what was wrong—she might not have seen anything at all. But she'd made a career out of reading witnesses' eyes and faces and there it was, lurking in the depths of those gorgeous amber eyes of his. He had feelings, deep feelings, for the woman who had convinced him to leave behind Boston and everything he knew in order to work in a low-income clinic in Atlanta.

Suddenly a lot of things she hadn't previously understood made sense.

No wonder Jack was so tormented. Not only had he lost the only career he'd ever known, he'd also lost the woman he loved. The fact that he was here anyway, willing to help her celebrate the next milestone in her life, spoke volumes about the kind of man he was. It didn't, however, look good in the boyfriend department.

Which was fine, she told herself viciously. It's not like this thing between them was serious or anything. They were friends with benefits, although she was currently doubting the friend part of that equation as friends didn't let friends fly blindly into situations like this.

Her fingers trembled against Jack's arm, and he turned to her, eyebrows raised. "You okay?" he asked. "I promise they don't bite."

"I'm fine."

And she was, she assured herself. The trembling was nothing. The ache in the pit of her stomach even less than nothing. She was being stupid letting this get to her. Obviously, Jack wasn't involved with Amanda, so how he felt about her shouldn't matter. It wasn't like Sophie was in love with him or anything. Or even like she'd planned on letting anything serious happen between them. Because she hadn't.

She'd taken herself out of the dating merry-go-round a long time ago and had no intention of getting back on. What she and Jack were doing now—was for kicks. For fun. She might not be interested in getting involved in a serious relationship with a man, but she was only thirty-five. Her body had needs that she'd ignored for far too long. Being with Jack was simply a way to relieve those needs.

God knew, she had enough issues of her own. The last thing she needed was to hook up with a guy who had a crush on another woman.

She wished he'd told her. That way she would have had time to prepare. And, more importantly, she wouldn't feel so damn stupid. Because that's all that hollow feeling was, she told herself determinedly. Embarrassment not hurt.

Blowing out a long breath, Sophie mentally put on her big-girl panties. Tilted her chin up, straightened her shoulders, readjusted her thinking and prepared to deal. Tonight would be difficult enough for Jack to deal with without her getting herself all upset. Doing that, would make things worse for him and she wasn't prepared to do that, not when he'd already had a crappy day. No matter what else had happened, no matter how annoyed she was with him right now, they were friends. And she wouldn't let him be embarrassed, wouldn't let him be hurt. Not after everything he'd already been through.

"Jack! There you are," Amanda called happily, as she rushed to meet them and pull them the final few steps to the large corner booth where she and her husband were sitting. "I was beginning to think you were going to stand us up."

"Sorry, traffic was bad," he lied smoothly, dropping a kiss on Amanda's cheek before reaching over to shake hands with Simon. "Good to see you, man."

"Good to see you, too," Simon responded in the clipped British accent that had once made Sophie swoon. "Amanda's been complaining because you haven't come by the house lately."

"Yeah, well, work and physical therapy are keeping me pretty busy."

"Plus babysitting," Sophie piped up, a little annoyed at how Amanda had twisted the knife. Simon was obviously oblivious to Jack's feelings for his wife, but there was no way Amanda could be. Not if they'd been friends as long as Jack told her they'd been. "Now that he's on nights, he's been watching my kids for me a few days a week."

"You didn't tell me that!" Amanda exclaimed. "That's wonderful. In the hospitals in Africa, they all clamor for Dr. Jack to take care of them. Jack is amazing with kids!"

"But not so great with introductions, obviously," Jack broke in. "Guys, this is my next-door neighbor Sophie Connors. Sophie, these are two of my closest friends. Dr. Amanda Jacobs and Simon Hart."

"It's good to meet you," she told them, firmly shaking their hands. "I've heard a lot about you from Jack."

"Really?" Amanda asked with a narrowed glare directed at her best friend. "Because he's been remarkably close-lipped about you, no matter how many questions I've asked since he said he was bringing a date."

Sophie started to come back with a snide remark, despite Jack's feelings for Amanda, but she couldn't do it. There was something genuine about the other woman. Something real and down-to-earth and yet vaguely injured. It was the same look Simon carried, the same look Jack had, and if she was being completely honest, it was the same look she sported, as well. She didn't know the specifics, but sometime, somewhere, fate had done a number on Amanda Jacobs.

The fact that she'd been able to come back from it so successfully, and so nicely, went a long way toward soothing Sophie's dislike of her. The fact that Amanda really did appear clueless of Jack's feelings—though she had a genuine affection for him—took Sophie the rest of the way. Dinner passed easily, with stimulating conversation, great food and fine wine for everyone but Amanda. As the night wore on, Sophie relaxed despite herself. She wanted to dislike Amanda, but she couldn't. The woman was too genuine. And Simon was wonderful, as well. Not smooth and charming like Jack—no, he had too many rough edges for that, but he was warm and open in his affection for his wife and his old friend.

No wonder Jack had come to this celebration dinner. Even if it hurt him, it would be impossible to turn his back on this couple and their happiness.

During a lull in her discussion with Simon about

the precarious state of dictatorships in the Middle East, she glanced at Jack, who was deep in conversation with Amanda about some medical procedure he didn't agree with. He looked earnest and intelligent and concerned.

The one thing he didn't look was happy. But then, if she had to watch the man she loved sitting with the woman he loved, she probably wouldn't be very happy, either...

JACK GLANCED UP to see Sophie staring at him. He started to smile, but there was a strange shimmer to her green eyes, one that hit him straight in the gut. Was she crying?

But then she grinned at him before turning to launch herself back into a spirited discussion with Simon and he told himself it must have been a trick of the light. She looked like she was having a great time. She'd certainly fit right in with his friends like she'd always been there.

"I like her," Amanda said softly, resting her hand on his forearm.

He braced himself for the old feelings to rip through him at her touch, for the pain of knowing she was lost to him forever to rear its ugly head like it so often did. Instead, there was barely a twinge, a deep-down contentment that Amanda's life was finally back on track. And his, while not on track, wasn't nearly as bad as it had been even a couple of weeks ago. That was thanks, in great part, to Sophie and her boys.

"I do, too. A lot."

"I can tell. And I have to admit, I'm glad. Maybe Sophie will be able to keep you from running straight back to the nearest war zone. God knows, I've never been able to."

"Because you were usually there right along with me."

"Well, there is that." She took a sip of her water. "But seriously, Jack, you look good. A lot better than when you showed up at the clinic a few weeks ago."

"Don't beat around the bush, Amanda. Call it like you see it."

"You know I always do. So, why don't you do the same. Seriously. How are you really doing?"

Silence stretched between them and he knew she was waiting for him to say something, but he didn't know what to say. Oh, he knew what she wanted to hear—that his hand was getting better and everything in his life was peachy.

But that wasn't the truth, and while he was great at putting on a smile and laying on the charm to cover a multitude of pain, he'd never been a big fan of straight-out lying. Especially not to his good friends.

With Amanda looking at him like that, though, he knew he wasn't going to get away with brushing her off with a funny anecdote. So he told her the truth, or as much as he was ready to tell anyone. "My leg's doing great. It's almost completely healed, and I'm just about done with physical therapy for it."

"That's good to hear." She didn't look impressed. "And your hand?"

"My hand is fine. It's going to take time." Which wasn't strictly the truth. There hadn't been any improvement in a couple of weeks, and his doctor thought he had reached a plateau. Hence the whole hedge-cutting debacle of the morning—his physical therapist thought that some heavy duty exercises might shock his body into responding, getting off this plateau, but he wasn't so sure.

"What kind of time?"

"We don't know yet." He tried to smile, but he could feel the strain in it. Sophie must have seen it, too, because she jumped in to save him.

"So, Amanda, are you going to find out if it's a boy or a girl? Or do you and Simon want to be surprised?"

The conversation shifted after that, to the baby and the nursery Amanda was hoping to put together and then on to funny stories about Sophie's two boys. He sat back and listened for most of it, as did Simon, but he would be lying to himself if he didn't say he liked the new bent in the conversation. Not just because it got him out of talking about his least favorite subject in the world, but also because it gave him a chance peek at family life, to see what he'd been missing all these years.

Not that he was in shape emotionally for anything resembling a family, but it was good to know that some babies in this world were being born into happy, healthy families. And that they were thriving. He hoped that this baby would be healthy. He was still haunted by the loss of Gabby, Amanda and Simon's first child and his goddaughter. Looking at them, seeing their excitement in the new baby, was wonderful. But lurking in their eyes, behind their smiles, was the knowledge that doing everything right still didn't guarantee a healthy child, as well as the fear that they would lose this one, too.

Dinner wrapped up around ten-thirty and as they were leaving the restaurant, Jack pulled Simon aside and congratulated him one more time on the baby. Then he asked how Amanda was doing, because he knew his old friend as well as she knew him, and despite her obvious joy at being pregnant again, he knew she was hurting, as well.

"I don't know," Simon told him. "I keep asking her to talk to me, but she's got everything locked up so tight inside that I figure it's just a matter of time before she shuts down again."

"Don't let that happen."

"I'm trying not to, but you know Amanda. She's so headstrong that she keeps everything inside until it's too late to help her. I'm hoping that if I keep at her, keep making sure that she talks about things even when she doesn't want to, that it will be enough."

Simon's words hit home, and though he knew the

other man was talking specifically about Amanda, Jack could feel the truth of them applied to himself, as well. He was doing the same thing as Amanda and it was a matter of time before everything blew up in his face.

After clapping Simon on the back and hugging Amanda, he looked up to see Sophie watching him. There was compassion in her eyes, but also a spark of anger that turned the deep green nearly phosphorescent. He wished he knew which emotion was directed at him, and what he'd done to deserve it.

CHAPTER FIFTEEN

THE RIDE HOME was an uncomfortable one. Sophie was perfectly polite, perfectly nice, but there was a distance between them that had, quite obviously, not been there before. It wasn't the end of the evening he'd been anticipating, and by the time he got back to their houses he was pretty much in a quandary.

He knew the way he'd expected the evening to end—with Sophie in his bed for a couple of hours before she went home to relieve her babysitter. He knew she'd anticipated it ending the same way, so he wasn't sure what had happened to change her mind. All he knew was that the cool, precise woman sitting next to him was a far cry from the hot, sexy one he'd come so close to making love to in the car before dinner.

As he pulled onto their street, he kept debating back and forth with himself. Did he pull into her driveway or did he pull into his own. By the time he made it to the front of her house, he still hadn't made a decision and it was frustrating in the extreme. He wasn't the sort to be crippled by indecision when it came to women and he really didn't appreciate that such a thing was starting now.

Finally he decided, what the hell. If there was something wrong she was going to have to tell him, because he wasn't a mind reader and after an evening of playing cat-and-mouse with Amanda, he was too tired for games. Especially ones that dealt with emotions.

With a grimace, he pulled into his driveway and waited for the sparks to fly. It didn't take long. Sophie took a deep breath as she gathered her clutch from the bottom of the car and reached for her door without waiting for him to come around to hold it for her.

"Would you like to come in, for a cup of coffee?" he asked as he met her near the front of the vehicle.

"You know what? I think I'm going to head in. It's been a long night and I'm tired. I'll see you tomorrow." She started to slip past him, but he grabbed her elbow with his good hand, then spun her around to face him even as he backed her up against the hood of his car.

"Do you want to tell me what's wrong?" he asked, even as his lower body sunk against hers.

"I told you. It's been a long night and—"

"Don't," he told her, his hand coming up to rest against the hollow of her throat. "Don't make excuses." Her pulse was hammering there, fast and heavy, and he didn't know if it was because she was nervous or if it was because she was angry. At least not until her eyes flashed at him and her hand came up to push him away from her.

"I understand why you did it, really, I do," she told him. "But I don't appreciate being used. If you'd told me—" Her voice broke, for the first time sending alarm skittering down his spine. "I still would have come with you, you know."

"Told you what?" he asked, baffled.

She made a noise deep in her throat and for a second he thought she was going to hit him. But Sophie was way too nice for that and she settled for brushing past him, leaving him empty-handed and confused.

He was prepared to let her go, to watch as she marched across the lawn and up the stairs to her house. He didn't like it, but he'd been around enough angry women in his life to know when to push and when to let them stew. This definitely seemed to be the latter situation.

But when she was only a few steps from her house, she turned around to face him again. He knew there was something she wanted to say—it was written all over her face—just as he knew she was too proper to shout it across their yards for the entire neighborhood to hear. Or at least he hoped she was, but he wasn't willing to stake his entire reputation on it.

Bum leg or not, he sped across the lawn to her. "Sophie, please," he said. "If I somehow hurt you, I'm really sorry. I certainly didn't mean it and I wish you'd give me a chance to make it up to you."

Sure, he was laying it on a little thick, but what

was the alternative? Go home to his empty house and toss and turn all night. It seemed cold comfort when, if he played his cards right, he could be making love to her for half the night instead.

"You didn't hurt me," she told him, but the hitch in her voice belied her words. "I thought… Why didn't you tell me? she repeated.

He threw his arms wide. "Tell you what?" he demanded, finally growing exasperated.

"That you were in love with Amanda."

She said the last words quietly, so quietly that he had to strain to hear them. But once he figured out what she was saying, once he understood, he felt like she'd driven an eighteen wheeler straight through him.

For long seconds he didn't say anything and neither did she. But the force of her words reverberated through the space between them, through the night air itself until they'd taken over his entire consciousness. Until they were all he could think about, all he could feel.

"I'm not," he finally told her hoarsely, and of all the responses he could have given her he got the feeling that this was the one that angered her the most.

"I'm not an idiot," she told him, marching straight back down the walkway to him. "I saw everything tonight."

His own anger kicked up. "Really? And what exactly did you see? Because, the truth is, there's nothing between Mandy and me but friendship and there never has been."

"Because she's in love with her husband, not because of any lack of feeling on your part."

The accusation sliced right through him. "You mean lack of effort on my part, don't you?"

She raised an eyebrow. "I don't know. Do I? You two looked awfully chummy to me tonight."

With that accusation, she'd gone too far and judging from the look on her face, he figured she probably knew it. He could see her debating on whether or not to back down, to apologize, but he was too fed-up to be impressed by it. With a shake of his head, he turned around and headed back to his house. He didn't need this shit on top of everything else in his life. He really didn't.

This is why he didn't do relationships, he fumed as he took the steps up to his house two at a time. Even when you thought you'd done nothing wrong, even when you were on your best behavior, they still bit you in the ass. It was ridiculous.

He was fumbling his key into his lock when he smelled her. Jasmine and cinnamon and a sweet, fresh smell that was uniquely Sophie. He almost ignored her, almost opened his front door, went inside and then closed it in her face. But that would solve nothing between him and despite his anger and his angst, he found that he very much wanted to solve the problem that had sprung up between them.

"I'm sorry," she said. "I had no right to go off on

you like that and I have no excuse for it. Except to say that I was blindsided when I realized what was going on tonight and I handled it badly. I had no right to expect anything from you and even less of a right to expect to be privy to your feelings. It's just—" She stopped, looking confused and unsure for the first time since he'd met her. "It's just that I care about you more than I expected to and I don't really know what to do about that."

She waited a few seconds after she finished, but when he didn't say anything, she sighed. "I'll go now." Then turned and headed back down the steps.

He caught her before she hit the third stair. "Yes, I love Amanda," he told her. "I have for more years than I can count. But I realized something tonight, when I was sitting there with you and her and Simon. I'm not in love with her and I'm not sure I ever was. Did I ever think I was? Yes. Way back when I was twenty-two and we were starting med school together. I was crazy about her. But I don't think you can hold something against me that happened fifteen years ago."

"I know what I saw, Jack. It wasn't fifteen years in the past."

Damn stubborn woman. She wasn't going to be happy until she got the whole sordid story out of him. And what did it say about him that he was willing to tell her? What did it say about her and the fact that, despite everything he'd told himself, he'd let her into his life?

He didn't know, but he would be damned if he spilled any more of his guts on his front porch when there was a perfectly civilized living room right inside his door.

With that thought in mind, he pushed the door open and then held it while she followed. "Can I get you a drink?" he asked, crossing to the bar that he hadn't bothered to stock with much more than a bottle of whiskey.

"I'm good, thanks."

He ignored her, pouring two tumblers of the stuff, neat, and shoving one into her hands. Then he drank it in a couple of long swallows. The burn grounded him, kept him focused. And made it easier for him to say what needed to be said.

"Maybe, in the past couple of years, I've entertained the thought that Amanda and I could be together. But even as I thought about it, dreamed about it, I knew she belonged with Simon, no matter how big a mess he'd made of their relationship. And trust me when I say, he made a huge damn mess.

"But I'm the one who called him to come get her when she nearly had a nervous breakdown, because no matter how I felt about her, I knew how she felt about him. So lately, when I fixated on her again— I think because, in my head, she represents everything I once was—I knew it wouldn't work out. That it couldn't work out. And that made her safe in a way no other woman could be, in a way I knew—from the second I laid eyes on you—that you couldn't be.

There's not a safe, comfortable bone in your body. Obviously, or you wouldn't expect me to stand here baring my soul to you after our first real date."

He stopped there, prayed he'd said enough for the night, because he didn't think he had it in him to share any more. It had been a hard night, one filled with revelations. First, in the car, with Sophie, when he'd realized her happiness, her satisfaction, was more important to him than his own. And then later, in the restaurant when he sat there, talking to Amanda, looking between her and Sophie, he'd known that the feelings he'd been harboring for Amanda had really been more about nostalgia and comfort than they ever were about real, passionate love. Like he'd told Sophie, in his head, Amanda represented the life he'd once had and the doctor he'd once been. But that person was long gone, and trying to recapture the past to make himself feel alive again, wasn't what he would exactly call a smart move.

Besides, not once had he ever imagined taking Amanda to bed—at least not in more than a decade. He'd thought it was because the shooting had messed everything up, including his libido, but the fact of the matter was that he couldn't keep his mind, or his libido, off the idea of having Sophie in his bed.

"I'm sorry if my perceived feelings for Amanda hurt you. That's the last thing I ever wanted to do."

He paused to look at her, to see how she was taking his grand confessional, but her face was blank, her beautiful, expressive eyes giving nothing away.

That's when he figured he'd failed, because the Sophie he knew was bursting with emotion nearly every second of every day.

He told himself he wasn't going to keep hammering the point home, that he'd told her everything he needed to about him and Amanda. That at some point she was going to have to trust him. But it was hard to stick to that when for the first time in a long time— maybe ever—his entire being was straining toward another person's. He wanted to hold her, wanted her to feel the same need for him that was rocketing through him for her.

And then she did something completely unexpected, so out of the realm of his expectations that for long seconds he could do nothing but stand there and stare at her in shocked desire.

Instead of giving up on him and walking away, she shimmied out of her sexy green dress, letting it fall on the entryway floor. She stood there, in front of him, wearing nothing but a sheer green bra and panty set and her gold stiletto heels.

And then she started walking toward him, hips swinging, breasts bouncing. It was more than enough to convince him that whatever soul-baring he'd done that night was completely and utterly worth it.

She stopped in front of him, looking more provocative than any woman had a right to. For a second, he was afraid he was going to embarrass himself and come right there. Sophie must have known what he was thinking, because she gave a wicked little laugh, even as she closed the last bit of distance between them and twined her arms around his neck. "Kiss me, Jack," she whispered.

He could do nothing but oblige.

Wrapping his arms around her, pressing that amazing body of hers tightly against him, he kissed her until he was drowning in her. Until he couldn't breathe, couldn't move, couldn't think without it being wrapped up in her.

And then he kissed her some more.

He wanted her on fire, wanted her burning with the same need that threatened to consume him. He wanted to slip past the defenses she'd erected between them tonight, wanted to go back to the way things had been between them the day before.

But that wouldn't work—for him or her—because his feelings for her weren't the same. They were bigger now, more complex, friendship a small part of everything that he was feeling. And while he wanted to continue being Sophie's friend, after tonight, he also wanted so much more.

Pulling away a little, he skimmed his mouth over her rounded cheeks and down the delicate skin of her jaw as the world around him began caving in. As his focus narrowed to the two of them and this one, perfect moment.

He wanted to take her higher than she'd ever been before. Craved it with everything inside of him. And when she reached for him, cupping his jaw in her hand and pulling his mouth back to hers, he knew he'd hit the jackpot.

With a groan, he slid his tongue inside her mouth, thrusting between her lips the way he wanted to thrust between her thighs. Demanding more and more but giving her everything he could, as well.

SOPHIE CRIED OUT at Jack's desire for her. His hands tightened around her as if he was afraid she would try to move away, but she wanted nothing more than to burrow against him and stay there for as long as he would let her.

She loved the feel of him, the way his talented tongue stroked over every inch of her mouth. The way his strong chest pressed so firmly against hers. Need raced through her, overwhelmed her, until she was desperate. It seemed like months, years, since she'd last had him instead of a little more than twenty-four hours.

Tangling her tongue with his, she sucked him fully into her mouth and stroked the bottom of his tongue with her own. He growled low in his throat while his hands plunged into her hair, holding her head firmly in place.

Sophie relinquished his tongue with a moan, tilting her head back until she could see his face. His eyes were so dark, his pupils so wide, that his beautiful irises had all but disappeared. "I need you," she whispered to him, taking his injured hand and placing it on her breast. "Please, make love to me."

It was all the invitation he needed as, breathing hard, he backed her across the entryway and down the hall to his room. Once there, he pressed her against the glass door that led to his patio and held her there as his lips ran over her neck and shoulders and down the curves of her arms to her elbows.

Wherever he touched, fire raced through her and she could tell he felt the same way. His breathing was harsh, his muscles tight, his arousal hard where it pressed against her.

His hands moved up, cupped her breasts and she gasped at how good he felt. Then he bent down, licked over first her right breast and then her left, so softly, so sweetly, that unexpected tears sprung to her eyes. She blinked them away, tried to concentrate on the moment and only the moment, but it was difficult. His every kiss, his every touch, was with complete reverence and care.

Then his mouth turned rougher, liquid flames licking their way from her nipples to her stomach, down her arms and legs until they coalesced at her aching sex.

"Jack, please." She moved against him, clutching and arching as she tried to convince him that she was ready.

He only laughed and pulled his mouth away completely, his breath a soft breeze over her aching nipples. She grabbed his head in her hands, tangled her fingers in all that silky hair of his as she tried to force his mouth up to hers.

"Don't tease me," she whimpered, arching against him. "I can't take it."

"Sweetheart, I haven't begun to tease you." He curled his tongue around her areola, sucked it into his mouth with a suction so strong he had her gasping.

"Did I hurt you?" he asked urgently, immediately softening the pressure.

"No, no, no!" The cry came from deep inside of her as she arched her back, pressed herself more deeply against him. When he took her again, this time nipping softly, she had to clench her teeth to keep from screaming.

"Take me!" she cried, not caring that she was begging, or that she sounded hot and needy and completely overwhelmed. She was all of those things, so why shouldn't Jack know? He was the one doing it to her after all.

She wanted him inside her, needed him inside her. Knew, if he didn't make a move soon she was going to do whatever it took to get him there.

"I am taking you," he whispered, his breath hot against her breast. But she was too out of control to understand what he was saying, too far gone to do anything but push against him, whimpering, pleading, begging for him to put her out of her misery.

But no matter what she did, he refused to be hurried. Instead he pushed her and pushed her until she was certain that she would fly apart into a million pieces. He licked and sucked and kissed and nibbled his way all over her body until she was on the brink of madness. Only then, when she was strung tight as a violin string, did he drop to his knees in front of her.

"Oh, please!" She couldn't stop the whimper that welled in her throat, any more than she could keep from twisting her hands in his hair. Rough, calloused hands parted her trembling thighs, and though he tried not to press it against her, she felt the slick, hard scar tissue that took up so much of his right hand.

She wanted to grab his hand, to bring it to her lips and kiss it, so that he would see that she didn't care, that she thought every part of him was beautiful. But she knew enough to know that he would never go for that. It would yank him out of the moment, rip him away from her, and that was the last thing she wanted right now.

"You're so beautiful, Sophie." He said the words to her in a dark whisper that sent shudders through every part of her. "So amazingly, unbelievably beautiful." He trailed a finger down her neck, over her shoulder, across her breast and nipple, down her stomach to the very center of her.

She trembled—at his touch and his words. No man had ever looked at her like he did, like he really did think she was beautiful and like he wanted to devour every part of her.

It made her happy and it made her sad, made her fall a little more deeply under his spell even as she worried that she was letting him take her too far, that she was giving him too much.

The thought came to her that this was a lot more than a friendly fling, a warning that she was going to be crushed when he chose to leave her for Africa. She knew she should listen to it, knew she should care, but right now she was drowning in the pleasure he brought her so that it was the only thing that mattered.

He was the only thing that mattered.

The thought made heat explode within her, shooting her arousal from hot to feverish in the blink of an eye. She could feel an orgasm welling powerfully within her and she stood there, shaking, while he brought her right to the brink with a few flicks of his tongue.

And then he was moving on, moving down, his lips skimming over the curve of her stomach, down the side of her hip. His tongue made little forays underneath her hip bone, soft, sweet touches that nonetheless lit her up like the Fourth of July. Sharp little nips that had her gasping for air and pleading with him to take her before she exploded.

HE WAS DROWNING in her, Jack thought, as he buried his face between Sophie's thighs. Sinking straight into her, into a place where nothing mattered but the two of them. She smelled delicious, like the rain and vanilla and the sweet magnolia tree that grew outside her window. He paused for a moment, pulled her scent deep inside himself, even as he stroked his thumbs closer and closer to the slick folds of her sex.

With each graze of his thumb she trembled more. With each clap of his hands, she took a shuddering breath. And when he moved forward, blowing one long, warm stream of air against her, she started to cry, to sob, her body spasming with even the lightest touch of his against it.

He was going to burst in flames, his erection so hard that he feared he might embarrass himself if he didn't get inside her soon. But he wasn't ready for it to end, wasn't ready to send either of them careening over the edge.

But she was coming apart, her body so sensitive and responsive that it awed him even as it made him shake.

"You're amazing," he muttered as he delivered one long lick along her beautiful sex. "So unbelievably gorgeous that I could—" He stopped as Sophie cried out, her hands clutching his hair as flames ripped through her. He kissed her a second time, and then a third, lingering on her most sensitive spot.

She sobbed as she hurtled over the edge, orgasm exploding through her body. He held her while she came, stoking the flames higher and higher until she was sobbing, her hands clutching his shoulders in an effort to pull him up and into her. Her need sent him over his own edge, and he stood in a rush. "I need to be inside you," he growled, as he carried her to the bed, turning her so that she lay face down across his comforter.

Skimming his mouth over her neck, he reached

between her legs to make sure that she was still ready for him. She was slick, swollen and so hot he shuddered with a desperate need to be inside her.

With a groan, he grabbed a condom from his nightstand and slid it on. Then he pulled her hips back, and with his knees shaking and body throbbing, he sank into her slowly.

She felt amazing, smooth and silk and so hot he feared she would burn him alive—but what a way to go. With her wrapped around him like a fist, her strong body quivering against his, he wanted nothing more than to stay like this forever. Working his way inside her as she found her way inside him. Taking all that she had to offer.

Sophie moaned as Jack entered her. Arching her back, she tried desperately to get as close to him as she possibly could.

He held her steady, his thrusts more gentle than she'd expected from the way he'd stoked the inferno between them. She struggled to press back against him, to take him more fully, but he held her steady.

"Jack, please!" she gasped.

He thrust hard against her and it felt so good to finally have all of him that she cried out. "Am I hurting you?" he asked through gritted teeth.

"No!" She tried to turn over, tried to take control, but he wouldn't let her. He kept moving against her, slowly, tenderly, gliding in and out of her again and again. The pleasure built and built until she was, unbelievably, once again on the edge.

Reaching behind her, she grabbed on to his hips and pulled him against her as hard as she could, wanting him as deep inside her as he could go.

He wasn't expecting it, and the move—along with the way she squeezed him deep inside of her—sent him careening over the edge. He brought her with him, into a powerful maelstrom of emotion and ecstasy that took everything she had to give and more.

In those moments, Jack was all around her, inside her. Not just her body, but every part of her. And that's when she knew why she'd been so upset at dinner, why it had bothered her so much that Jack had feelings for Amanda. Not because they were friends and he'd let her walk into the situation blind, not because she was sick of coming in second to somebody, something, else. But because somehow, in the middle of her project, she had fallen head over heels in love with Jack.

CHAPTER SIXTEEN

ALMOST AS SOON as the realization came to her, Sophie tried shoving it back to wherever it came from. No good would come from her acknowledging her feelings for Jack. She knew that very well. Eventually, he would leave, would head back to Africa or Boston or anywhere else, and she would be left here to pick up the pieces of her broken life…again.

The thought frightened her, had her shoving out from beneath him while he was still gasping for air. She didn't care, though, not while panic was a living, breathing monster inside of her. She couldn't love Jack. She couldn't.

She started searching for her underwear. She knew her dress was in the foyer where she'd dropped it, but if she went home without a bra on, she was never going to hear the end of it from Sabrina.

"Hey, what's your hurry?" Jack asked, springing out of bed and padding lightly over to her. "I thought we were going to cuddle this time, while both of us were awake."

She smiled, she couldn't help it, not when he was wearing that charming grin that had melted her knees from the very first time she saw it. He really was a good guy. A little lost, a little confused, but who wouldn't be after what he'd gone through? That was the problem though. As lost and confused as he was, there was no room for her own doubts. Her own fears. Which meant, much as she wanted to stay with him and give this a shot, there was no way she was going to be able to do it. They weren't going to be good for each other, and that meant there was no way he could be good for her boys.

Still, when he held his arms out to her, wearing nothing but that silly grin, she couldn't walk away. Not yet. Not before she held him one more time. Which was why, when everything inside of her screamed at her to run—everything that was but her foolish, traitorous heart—she let him pull her against him in a light embrace. His lips skimmed over her hair and across her ear, and though she knew he meant the caress to be comforting and not arousing, she felt an answering response deep inside her. A response that yearned for more than simply a physical connection with him.

That, too, scared her, the way Jack had waltzed in here and basically claimed ownership of her body. Oh, he would never do anything to hurt her physically, or scare her—she knew she was safe with him that way. But this strange vulnerability, this openness he'd called forth from her, made her want nothing so much as to run and hide.

None of her previous relationships—no matter

how solid or fleeting—had prepared her for the wealth of emotion inside her. None of it had prepared her for what it would be like to love Dr. Jack Alexander.

She wasn't going to run though, no matter how much she wanted to curl up and lick her wounds. That simply wasn't an option, namely because she couldn't stand the idea of him knowing how stupid she'd been. She didn't want him to feel obligated toward her or the boys in any way nor did she want him to feel sorry for her. She wouldn't be able to stand that. And the number one reason she was going to walk out of here with head held high—she knew Jack didn't feel the same way about her. Understandably. He was too busy fighting his demons, too busy trying to be the man he once was, to truly live as the man he was becoming. And that, she lamented, was the biggest shame of them all.

But that didn't mean she was going to stick around and let him see how crazy about him she was. She knew pride was a deadly sin and that it went before a fall, but, honestly, Sophie couldn't bring herself to care. Not now, when everything she was, everything she'd made for herself, was on the line.

She had a vision of herself waltzing out of the room, head up, eyes front, a big smile on her lips. It would be fake, but Jack didn't have to know that. Except…she could tell from the look on his face that her abrupt departure was setting off all his warning bells just as surely as throwing herself at his feet and declaring her undying love would.

She'd been too quick, too frantic. She needed to slow down, relax a little, rein in the panic. Surely she could do it if she gritted her teeth and bore it for a little while longer.

Leaning forward, she brushed a kiss across Jack's jaw, then forced a smile she was far from feeling.

"I need to get home," she told him. "I hadn't realized how late it was getting and Sabrina has plans early in the morning."

He nodded, though his eyes were still watchful. "Okay. Let's get dressed and I'll walk you back."

"You don't have to do that," she said with a laugh so high it hurt her ears. "I can find my own way next door."

His eyes narrowed, and she realized, not for the first time, that Jack really was a force to be reckoned with. "I'm not sure what kind of men you're used to, Sophie, but I see my dates home."

Admitting defeat, she threw up her hands. "Okay, okay. I was trying to be helpful." She grabbed her underwear and pulled it on.

"Yeah, well, don't," he told her.

As she was slipping on her shoes, she noticed the necklace she'd been wearing to dinner crumpled on the floor. It must have fallen off when they'd been making love. Stooping down, she picked it up and tried to fasten it around her neck again, but her hands were shaking too badly to do the clasp.

"Do you need help?" Jack asked, wrapping an arm around her waist from behind and nuzzling her neck a little.

She tried to stay strong, but the feel of his lips against her nape had her melting into him before she could steel herself. She didn't know how long they stood there, bodies pressed together, Jack's lips skimming over the sensitive skin of her neck, behind her ear, the top of her shoulder. But when she couldn't take it anymore, when she knew one more second would have her flinging herself on the bed and begging for a repeat performance, she pulled herself away. Handed him the necklace.

"Thanks. The boys gave it to me for my birthday last year and I'm paranoid about not losing it."

"No problem," he said, but as he draped it around her neck, again from behind, she realized that there was a really huge problem—she'd been too wrapped up in her own issue to notice it.

The clasp on the necklace was tiny and there was no way Jack was going to be able to work it with his injured hand. No way at all.

"Never mind," she told him, pulling at the pendant from the front. "Now that I think about it, I'm going to take it off again when I get home. I can put it in my purse."

Jack stiffened against her. "I can fasten a damn necklace, Sophie."

Terrific. She closed her eyes, blew out a breath. Now she'd hurt his feelings. "I know you can, Jack."

So she stood there and waited while he tried to open the clasp. Once, twice, then again and again. It was one of the most awful experiences of her life. Tears bloomed in her eyes, but she forced her breathing to remain even. Forced herself to breathe through her mouth when the tears clogged her throat.

She could feel his frustration mounting, knew he was getting toward the breaking point, but she also knew she couldn't be the one to say enough. He'd never forgive her for it, never forgive himself.

Finally, after a few minutes had passed, he gave up, handed the necklace to her. She wanted to say something, to assure him that it wasn't a big deal, but she knew that to him, it was. She could see it in his squared-off shoulders and the rigid lines of his back. Could see it in the eyes that would no longer meet hers.

He dressed quickly after that, as did she, and before she knew it they were standing on her front porch. Sabrina had left the light on, so Sophie could see the angry set of Jack's jaw. Angry at her, angry at himself, she didn't know. Probably a little bit of both, considering the emotional roller coaster their date had become.

Leaning forward, she brushed her lips softly against his, because she simply couldn't resist. She wanted to wrap her arms around him, to hold him to her even though she knew that doing so would only end up hurting the both of them.

But she couldn't leave him like this, either. She

couldn't walk away when he was so angry with himself over something so stupid. "Jack," she whispered as she placed her hand on his chest. "Please, don't do this."

"Don't you do it, Sophie. You were the one running out of my bedroom like your hair was on fire tonight, so don't suddenly feel sorry for me because of that damn necklace. I don't need your charity." His voice was low, venomous, filled with more rage than Sophie had ever heard from him.

"It wasn't like that," she told him, pain slicing through her with each second that passed. She'd known this was inside him, known that he was angry and hurt and horrified, but when she'd decided weeks ago to try to help him, she'd planned on doing just that. She hadn't known that she was going to be the catalyst to break him completely, the one who would finally crack his self-control and have all that vitriol spilling over the sides.

"It was exactly like that. I don't know what happened tonight, don't know what I did to make you so upset when we were making love. I thought we were together in it."

"We were, Jack. I swear. I loved every second of being with you."

He looked at her, his beautiful whiskey-colored eyes a dull brown now that the charm and wit were gone from them. "I could tell."

"Damn it, Jack, don't do this to yourself. Don't let my neuroses make you feel bad about yourself. I'm sorry I freaked out like that, sorry I tried to make a run for the door. And I'm sorry, so sorry, about that stupid necklace. If I could do it all over again, I would never have asked you."

He froze at the last, his expression wiped clean of everything that had been there before. The anger. The confusion. The joy from earlier. It was all gone and in its place was a cold mask she didn't know how to penetrate. "That's the problem, isn't it?" he asked her. "No one thinks they can ask me anything. No one can count on me for anything anymore."

"That isn't true!"

He tapped her fist, where the necklace was still clenched. "Sure it is, Sophie. You're too nice to tell me so to my face."

Desperate, devastated, horrified at the prospect that in one night she had carelessly ruined everything Jack had been working toward, Sophie flung herself against him. For the first time since they'd met, his hands didn't come up to steady her, his arms didn't wrap around her. He stood there like a statue, like he had actually turned to stone.

She wouldn't let it bother her. Standing on her tiptoes, she wrapped her arms around his neck and pressed her lips to his.

He still didn't respond, until she opened her mouth and licked her tongue over the seam of his lips from corner to corner.

With a groan, he brought his hands up to cup her

bottom and lift her so that she was pressed tightly against him.

Then he kissed her, really kissed her, until it once again felt like the rest of the world was far away. Like it was just the two of them in this one, perfect moment. She knew it was going to end, knew it couldn't last, but she clung to him, fingers tangled into his shirt for as long as he would let her.

They kissed and kissed and kissed, until she was breathless and shaky and aroused—so aroused—all over again. Then she moaned, and it broke the spell. His hands dropped and he stepped away from her, his face blank once again. She took a perverse satisfaction in the fact that he was as out of breath as she was.

Reaching a hand up to his face, she caressed his cheek. "Good night, Jack."

He inclined his head, his eyes as unreadable as that blank face he wore. "Goodbye, Sophie."

She slipped inside and locked the door. The house was dark. Sabrina—who was spending the night in the guest room—was already asleep. Which was a good thing, Sophie told herself, because her friend had a nose like a bloodhound when it came to emotional upsets. There was no way Sophie would ever be able to hide how messed up she was from Sabrina.

And she wanted desperately to hide it from her friend, for her sake and for Jack's. After what she'd done to him, there was no way she would ever talk about what had happened to anyone. He didn't deserve that. Feeling a sob well up inside of her—which was stupid, as she was the one who had freaked out and started them down this path—she took a deep breath, forced it back down.

She started up to bed, where she planned to pull the covers over her head and pretend the past half an hour had never happened, when she glanced out the window and saw Jack still standing on his own front porch, staring at her house. He looked so completely alone that the sob burst out of her chest, despite her best efforts to stifle it. It was followed by another and another, until she was crying in earnest.

She headed back down the stairs to the front door, not sure what she was going to say, knowing only that she couldn't leave him like that. But before she could call to him, he turned around and headed inside, turning off the porch light before he even got his front door closed.

As he did, she was the one left alone in the dark.

ANOTHER AFTERNOON passed without Sophie sending the boys over. Which he totally should have expected, but somehow he hadn't. And even after he thought he'd been inoculated against the pain of losing Sophie—and the boys—in one fell swoop, it turned out that he wasn't.

He didn't know why she hadn't sent them over, any more than he knew why she had hired one of those expensive babysitter services she couldn't afford. He probably should have called that first evening, four nights ago, when she'd gotten home from work. Told her that he was still willing to watch Noah and Kyle.

But he hadn't, because a part of him had wondered if she'd hired another babysitter because she didn't trust him to be able to take care of the boys. And why should she, when he couldn't do some of the most simple tasks around?

Still, it hadn't kept him from standing in the shadows and watching as the boys played outside in the yard. The new babysitter kept them in the backyard, but if he watched from an upstairs window he could still see them. And if he hung out in the living room around six o'clock every night—for no particular reason—he could glance up and see Sophie coming home, looking sexy as hell in her suits with their short, tight skirts.

That meant she'd been in court all week, he remembered, because pantsuits meant office time. It was strange how he remembered these little details, all these little things about her when he'd never bothered to remember them about anyone else.

Or maybe it wasn't so strange as he'd never felt this way about someone else. He thought about Sophie all the time, dreamed about making love to her, waited for her to get home with the eagerness of a puppy. And sometimes, when she got home and turned to look at his house, it took every ounce of self-control he had not to go to her.

The only thing holding him back was the fact that

he had no idea what kind of reception he would get. She was the one who had freaked out on him, after all, the one who had tried to leave his house so fast he'd feared her hair had caught fire.

At the time he'd been worried that he'd hurt her with his lovemaking, that he'd been too rough with her and that was why she was having nothing to do with him.

He'd tried to be gentle that last time, despite the need for her that had shredded his control, had been doing a pretty good job of it—he thought—until she'd pushed him over the edge. He knew he'd gotten rough then, and he was sick with the idea that he had somehow frightened or hurt her.

He wanted to talk to her, to apologize if he had indeed done something to scare her. And if he hadn't, then it meant something else had upset her. Something big. And the only thing he could think of— besides the Amanda thing, which he was sure they had dealt with before making love—is that his hand had bothered her. Disgusted her.

Usually he was so careful not to use that hand, and if he did, he tried not to touch her with anything but the fingers so she wouldn't have to feel the scar tissue. But that night he hadn't been careful. He'd held her the way he'd wanted, touched her the way he'd always wanted to. And then she had freaked out.

Plus, on Saturday, when he'd been making love to Sophie, he'd been leaning on his hands and his right hand had given out. He didn't know why, except that it must not have been ready to support all his weight. He'd stumbled, would have fallen against Sophie if she hadn't caught him. Add to that the debacle over the necklace and was it any wonder he hadn't marched over to her house and demanded that she talk to him? He wasn't a coward but he wasn't a glutton for punishment, either. If she couldn't deal with his hand, then fine. It was better to find that out now than to find it out later. Not that he actually expected her to be able to—God knew he had had a damn hard time accepting it and he didn't have a choice.

Still as he watched her pull her car in the drive, watched her turn to look at his house, he once again contemplated going over there. What could it hurt? he wondered. Besides his pride? Maybe he'd see if the kids wanted to get an ice cream or something.

But then he glanced at his watch and knew he would never do it. His shift started in forty-five minutes and with Atlanta traffic, it would take him a good half an hour to get from his house to the clinic. Not that he couldn't be late, if he really needed to be, but—

No. He shook his head, annoyed beyond belief with himself and the small part of him that kept hoping. Kept dreaming. Sophie had shown him how she'd felt in no uncertain terms. It was time for him to live with that.

Annoyed beyond belief—with himself and his foolish hopes and fears—he dressed for work quickly before slamming out of the house. After negotiating the traffic from hell, he finally blew into the clinic five minutes late and in a truly lousy mood. By the time he made it to the first exam room, he'd snapped at Amanda, pissed off Lucas and made one of the nurses cry. Definitely not his most impressive moment, if he did say so himself.

He took care of the patient—a little kid with strep throat—without getting anyone else mad at him, though it was touch and go for a while there. Moved on to a second patient and then a third before Amanda finally managed to corner him next to the coffeepot. That's what he got for not sleeping and needing a crutch. A lecture from the woman he least wanted to get a lecture from.

"So, Jack, how's it going?" she asked as she poured herself a cup of coffee he knew she wasn't going to drink.

"Fine," he said, taking a big sip of his own coffee while feigning nonchalance. All he got was a burned tongue for his trouble.

"Glad to hear that," she said with a smile. "How's physical therapy?"

"Fine."

"Any doctor's appointments lately?"

"No."

"And how about Sophie. How is she?"

"She's fine."

"Hmm. How about the pain levels? Are your pain meds taking care of—"

Finally, he had enough of her poking and prodding and exploded. "If you want to know what's wrong with me, why don't you ask me instead of dancing around the subject like you're freakin' Tinkerbell?"

She had the gall to laugh. "Tinkerbell. Hmm, I like it. As for the rest, fine. What the hell is wrong with you?"

He shrugged. "I don't know. Everything's getting way out of hand."

"Everything?" she asked. "Or one thing in particular?"

"I'm not going to sit here and play semantics with you, Amanda."

"Sure you are. Because if you go back out there and make another nurse cry, Lucas is going to lose his patience. And that is never a good thing."

He lifted an eyebrow at her. "Am I seriously supposed to be afraid of Lucas?"

"No, of course not. But that doesn't mean you get to treat the entire staff like shit, either. I know you're having a rough time. I get that, but seriously, that's enough wallowing. Get over yourself."

It was on the tip of his tongue to tell her to go to hell, that she'd nearly wallowed herself into a mental institution a year ago, but he bit the comment back at the last second. Amanda wasn't pulling her punches, but she wasn't hitting below the best, either. And neither would he.

But before he could think of a suitable response, she ended up going where he'd wanted to for him.

"Yes, I am very aware of the fact that I have no room to talk. Yet, I'm going to anyway. Because you did the same thing for me a year ago. I didn't appreciate it then, but you saved my life—we both know that."

"I'm in no danger of dying, Amanda."

"Yeah, well, you're in no danger of living either, and I'm sick of watching it."

"This time, I'm not the one backing off."

"Oh, yeah?" The annoyed look faded from her eyes for the first time that morning. "I thought Sophie had enough guts to stick around."

"Yeah, I did, too. But I guess not."

"So what are you going to do about it?"

"Nothing. What can I do? Either she wants to be with me or she doesn't."

"Don't you mean, either she loves you or she doesn't?"

"Hey," he said, alarmed. "Who said anything about love?"

Amanda snorted. "Yeah, right. Because your panties are in this big of a wad because you want to sleep with her. You forget, I know you, Jack. Better than you know yourself sometimes."

He thought of the feelings he'd harbored for her for years, how she'd never seemed to have a clue. "Oh, really? You think you know everything about me?"

"I know enough. I know you're smart and brave and honest—sometimes to a fault. So why aren't you being honest with yourself right now?"

"I am being honest! She doesn't want me."

"What you're being, is cowardly. You've turned into a total chicken, Jack."

"I am not."

"Are so."

"Really? Are we five now?" He looked down his nose at her.

"Whether you want to admit it or not, you're scared. Scared of going to Africa, scared of giving it a shot with Sophie, scared of never being able to be a decent doctor—"

"I am a much better than a decent doctor, thank you!" he said, completely insulted. And realized, too late, that he'd walked right into Amanda's trap. Damn it. He hated when she did that.

"Well, one out of three's not bad." She smirked at him. "But you see what I'm saying, right?"

He did. For the past three and a half months, he'd been in the middle of an identity crisis. Those shooters had taken a lot more from him than his ability to be a surgeon. They'd taken his confidence, his belief in himself, pretty much his entire purpose for living. Was it any wonder then that he hadn't been able to figure out which way was up? Hadn't been able to find his way out of the hole he had dug for himself? He'd let a bunch of war criminals—uneducated, heartless thugs—dictate how he thought about himself and the world he lived in.

Which was, as Amanda had so eloquently put it earlier, total bullshit. And it was going to stop now.

It was time for him to stop being a coward and either figure out what he was going to do with this life of his or give up all together.

Surprisingly, he was for figuring it out, even if it meant he got his ass kicked.

"Thanks," he told Amanda sincerely. "I needed the ass-kicking."

"You did," she agreed. "But it's nothing you haven't done for me. I'm not as brutal about it."

"You say that because you're not on the receiving end this time around."

"You poor baby. How will you ever survive."

"You could say you're welcome, you know. Since I said thank you."

"You're welcome," she said with an exasperated roll of her eyes.

He glanced around the crowded waiting room, glanced back at Amanda. "Go," she said with a smile. "I'll cover for you."

CHAPTER SEVENTEEN

SOPHIE SETTLED ON the couch with a glass of wine and the remote control, the entire evening stretching before her. Normally she'd be thrilled with the turn of events—her boys only spent the night at their paternal grandparents' one night a month, after all—but now that this month's sleepover was here, all she could do was wallow in her own loneliness.

She'd done the right thing running away from Jack the other day. She kept telling herself that over and over again. Yet, that didn't make her feel any better. She wasn't sure that anything could, to be honest. Which was why she'd tried so hard to avoid this love thing, to begin with.

She'd known better. After learning at an early age that emotional attachments were not things that worked out—she'd managed to coast through life without ever really giving her heart to anyone. At least not to anyone but her two boys. And then Jack had come along with his charming grin and surly undercurrent and swept her off her feet. It would be laughable if it wasn't so pathetic. Little Sophie Connor, from the wrong side of Atlanta, in love with a

Harvard doctor. And stupid enough to think, even for a minute, that things could work out.

Disgusted with herself and the whole world, she drained her glass of wine and then poured herself a second. As she did, she ignored the twinge of motherly guilt deep inside herself. There was no one here. If she wanted to get drunk on red wine and have a pity party then that was exactly what she was going to do. Pathetic, no doubt. But sometimes pathetic was all a girl could manage.

Flipping on her television, she passed a romantic comedy, a horror movie, a comedy and finally settled on a tear-jerking drama. If she was going to wallow, then damn it she was really going to wallow. And in the morning, when she was fighting a wine hangover and cursing the fact that her head felt like it was going to explode, she was going to pack all this sentiment, all this unrequited love of hers away and never pull it out again.

She was halfway through the movie—and the bottle of wine—when a knock sounded at her door. She was sorely tempted to ignore it, after all the only people she wanted to see were currently eating pizza and ice cream at their grandparents' house. But when the knocking didn't work, whoever was out there started leaning on the bell. And it was hard to wallow properly when one couldn't even hear the movie one was using to do it.

Pissed off and already a little tipsy, she poured herself a third glass of wine and then walked to the door, glass in hand. Whoever was on the other side of the door was going to get a piece of her mind. Didn't they know the rules—that you never disturbed a woman when she was trying her best to get over a broken heart?

She had a whole speech prepared by the time she flung the door open, and was looking forward to delivering it, short though it may be. But the second she saw Jack, her entire brain froze. Just shorted out so that she could think of nothing to say. Nothing to do that didn't involve standing here, staring at Jack like he was a cross between Santa Claus and a serial killer.

"Sophie," he said, somehow managing to sound as nervous as she felt. Which was ridiculous. She was the one who had thrown herself at him, who—after everything—had tried to hang on. And he was the one who had walked away. The one who had stayed away for nearly an entire week.

She went to slam the door shut in his face, probably would have succeeded if he hadn't been quick enough to stick his foot next to the door wall and knock it back open.

"Please," he said, reaching for her. "Give me a chance to talk to you."

She scrambled back before he could touch her. If he did, if he laid a finger on her and she felt the warm strength of him against her, she would be lost. She knew it, as surely as she knew that today was Friday.

"Go away, Jack," she told him, even as he let himself into the house, closing the front door quietly behind himself. "I don't want you here."

Pain fluttered across his face, and she realized in astonishment that the coldness he'd shown her in his bedroom was gone. In its place was the Jack she remembered. The one who smiled and laughed and hurt. Watching her angry words inflict pain made her wonder which one was worse.

"I know. You've made that obvious." He crossed to her carefully, his hands down by his side. "I promise I won't touch you if you don't want me to."

"I don't want you to."

Here came the ripples of pain again, but this time he made no move to hide them from her. "Fair enough. But will you hear me out?"

"I don't think so." She shook her head, kept backing up. "I think it's better the way it's been. No touching. No talking. No having anything to do with each other."

"Why?"

"Excuse me?"

"Why is that better?" He moved closer again, and this time she decided to hold her ground. It was stupid, because the second his hand reached out to caress her cheek, he had her. And he knew it.

"Why is it better for us to be apart than together?" he whispered, leaning down so that his lips were only an inch or so from her ear.

"Why is it better for us to ignore each other's existence instead of spending time together when it's what we both want?" His lips skimmed over her cheek, pausing along the way to nibble at her jawline.

"Why is it better to deny us what we both want." He cupped her cheek, turning her head so that her lips met his in a kiss so sweet, so tender, that it frightened her all the way down to her soul. Yet she was helpless to pull away, helpless to kick him out. Helpless to do anything but kiss him back even as she tried to absorb him deep inside herself.

He took advantage of her weakness, used it to walk her across the room and press her against the back wall of the foyer, never once lifting his mouth from hers.

She couldn't breathe, couldn't think. A part of her brain screamed at her to stop this, warned her that she was going to get hurt, that this wasn't going to end well, but she couldn't seem to care. It felt too good to be held by Jack again after days of being alone.

Amazingly, that was the thought that gave her the strength to pull away. It had never bothered her to be alone before and the fact that it suddenly did now was a huge problem. What happened if she got out of the habit? If she started relying on Jack only to have him pull another disappearing act? A little voice in the back of her head reminded her that she, too, had tried to disappear. That she was the one who had actually cut and run first.

She did her best to ignore it, to concentrate on the hurt she'd felt ever since he'd walked away from her on her front porch, but she couldn't do it. Not when she looked up and into his eyes, which were filled with the same fear of rejection that she knew was reflected in her own.

"What are we doing to each other?" she whispered, pressing her hands against her throbbing lips. She could still feel him there, still taste him.

"Making each other miserable," he told her, "because we're both too afraid to give the other one a chance."

"I gave you a chance." The words were out before she even knew she was going to say them.

"And I gave you one, but here we are anyway."

"You need to go," she told him.

"I miss you, Sophie. I miss the boys and the time I used to spend with all of you. I miss holding you and loving you. And I miss who I am when I'm with you."

"Who is that?"

"Someone who remembers the good parts of life. Who doesn't always dwell on the things he can't change, and who enjoys being a part of the ones he can. Someone who realizes that there is a place for him in the world, though it isn't the one he originally intended. Someone's who's happy." His voice trailed off to a whisper. "Someone who loves you."

"Don't say that," she told him, her voice shaky. "Don't say that to me unless you mean it."

"I love you, Sophie. Why is that so hard for you to believe?"

"Because no one ever has. Not really. I mean, Noah and Kyle love me, but they're the only ones.

"My mom gave me to foster care when I was two. I never knew my dad. I lived in a bunch of foster homes until I was eighteen. They cared more about the money than they did me."

"What about your husband?"

"Jeff cared about me. I know that. Just like I cared about him. But we both had our reasons for getting married and they didn't have much to do with love." She paused, then wiped her palms against her jeans like she was suddenly nervous. "Which is why you can't tell me that. Not if you don't mean it. I can't take it. I can't—"

She couldn't say anymore because Jack's mouth was on hers and this time he wasn't letting go. He kissed her until they were both gasping for air, and when he pulled away it was to mutter, "I love you" and drag air into his oxygen-deprived lungs before he came right back and kissed her some more.

When they needed air one more time, he took to pressing kisses all over her. On her forehead, her cheeks, her collarbone, her shoulder. The curve of her elbow, her wrist, her shoulder blade. And with each kiss he whispered the words she was determined not to want, but that she was finding out she desperately needed.

Tears bloomed in her eyes, spilled over, and for the first time she made no move to hide them from

Jack, who leaned forward and caught them with his lips, slowly kissing all evidence of her sorrow away.

"Don't cry, sweetheart," he murmured. "Please don't cry."

"I don't know how to do this," she whispered to him. "I don't know how to be what you want me to be. I don't care about your hand. I know you think I do, but it doesn't matter to me. It never has."

HERE IT WAS. The moment of truth. He could either believe her, that his hand wasn't the obstacle between them—between him and the rest of the world—that he thought it was, or he could keep going down the road he was on, until his entire life lay in ruins before him.

Before he'd met Sophie, the choice would have been an easy one. He couldn't have anyone, couldn't have believed that it wasn't as horrific and awful to the rest of the world as it was to him.

But as she held his hand and pressed soft kisses to the center of it, directly over his scar, he didn't pull away. Didn't wince. He sat there and took the love and affection that she was attempting to give him.

Would it be enough? he wondered. There were a lot of difficulties coming up in his future, including more surgeries if he didn't start responding better to physical therapy. Could he really believe that none of that mattered to her? That she didn't care about having a whole, healthy lover or husband? That she accepted him the way he was?

As she cuddled into him, pressing one of her beautiful breasts against his palm, he realized that this too was an easy decision. Because he loved Sophie, he had to trust her. And because she loved him—he knew she did though she hadn't said it yet—she would trust him, as well.

The thought overwhelmed him, filled him up from the inside, so that all the rage and fear and self-pity was burned away by the wonder of his feelings for her. He wanted to love her forever, to cuddle her and cherish her and make love to her all at the same time. And all for the rest of her life. Nothing else mattered, only that she was his.

"Jack?" Her sweet, sexy voice flowed over him like honey. "Are you sure?"

For the first time in three long months, he was sure. Sure of her, sure of himself, sure of the family they would find a way to build together. "I'm positive," he said, bending his head to once again take her mouth with his.

They stayed that way for long moments, kissing and touching and holding. Making up for the last, long days when they'd done without each other. Needing her, loving her, he pulled away to look in her eyes, praying that he would see a little of what he was feeling reflected in her eyes.

But when she opened her eyes, when she looked at him with her gorgeous green irises glowing in the lamplight, he saw so much more. Yes, he saw the love she had for him, but he also saw the need she couldn't hide, a need combined with affection that somehow exactly mirrored his own feelings—it melted him like nothing else could have.

Leaning forward, he once again took her mouth with his own, using his lips and tongue to arouse her—to soothe her—in a way he never had before. Not with Sophie and not with any other woman. He wanted her, God did he want her, but even more overwhelming than the desire blasting through him was the tenderness he felt for her. The softness she brought to him, the sense of peace when he had spent so long being restless and unsure of himself and the world around him.

He nipped at her lower lip, reveling in the sexy moan she didn't even try to stop. Sucked it into his mouth in an effort to ease the confusing rush of feelings tearing at his insides.

She went wild, her lush, lithe body bucking against him even as her hands clenched on his hips in an effort to hold him against her. She wrenched her mouth from his, unbuttoned his shirt as she skimmed her mouth down his neck and over his shoulder. He wanted to grab her then, to pull her over him and bury himself deep inside of her. But she deserved more than that, they deserved more than that, and he was determined to make love to her with the slow tenderness he knew she needed. It wasn't easy, though, and he shuddered with the effort it took to restrain himself.

But this moment, this night after one of the worst

weeks of his life—after the worst period of his life—
meant more to him than a desperate drive for satisfaction ever could. Sophie was his and he wanted to
show her that being with him didn't always have to
be flash and fire, didn't always have to be a struggle
for her to find her balance.

Reaching up, he cupped her face in one of his
hands and looked at her. From the little lines just
starting at the corner of her glorious eyes to the small
scar that ran along the edge of her jaw to the random scattering of freckles that decorated her nose,
he memorized her. Pulled her face, pulled her, deep
inside of himself where he could hold on to her when-
ever the reality of his injuries started crashing in
on him.

And she let him. Instead of struggling against him
or ducking her head or trying to move things along
faster, Sophie lay there and let him look. Lay there
and watched him as intently and tenderly as he was
watching her.

When he couldn't take it any longer, when his
need to be inside her was nearly overwhelming, he
stripped her slowly. Kissed and nuzzled and touched
every part of her body. And then he moved so that
he covered her. So that every part of her body was
covered by every part of his. Not to dominate, but
to feel every part of her. Not to try to control, but to
try to show her how much he adored her.

Bending forward, he kissed the softness of her
lips, the corners of her mouth. Traced his tongue

along her full bottom lip, lingering at the cute little indention in the center of her lopsided upper lip. She was like the richest, smoothest velvet, so much softer and sweeter than he ever imagined a woman could be. So much hotter than he had dreamed his wife would be. And she would be his wife, even if she hadn't agreed yet. On everything else he could compromise, but not on this. He wanted a family with her. He wanted everything with her.

Her hands clutched at him, tried to pull him closer, but he clasped them in his own, kissing each of her fingers. He wanted to be gentle this time, to give her the tenderness she deserved. But the second she moved against him, he was lost. Lust rose, sharp and terrible and all-consuming. He ignored it, beat it down, kissed her some more. He was unwilling to give up her lips, unable to break the connection when everything inside of him clamored to be a part of her. To make her a part of him.

He didn't lift his mouth until she whimpered, gasped for air. Only then did he relinquish her lips, skimming his own down her cheek and over the long, graceful curve of her neck to the delicate bones of her shoulders. How could she be so fragile and yet so strong?

Then he forgot everything but the ecstasy of being with her as he licked and kissed his way over every inch of her body one more time. He explored the curve of her shoulder, the hollow of her throat, the back of her knee. Then tickled her ribs with his tongue before moving between her legs and tasting her. Feasting on her. Claiming her.

He slid his tongue over her sex, once, twice, loving the spicy scent and taste of her. Slipped inside of her and stroked her from the inside as her hands clutched at his hair, his shoulders.

Ran his tongue over and around the hard button of her clit as she sighed and moaned.

And then, with a quick flick of his tongue and a stroke of his fingers, he brought her to climax. Pulling back, desperate to see her, he stroked his thumb over her, intensifying Sophie's orgasm even as he watched her take her pleasure. Her back bowed, her hips moved languorously against his thumb, and her skin flushed a pretty pink that called to him, urging him to take her. To take all of her.

"Jack!" It was a plea and they both knew it. "I want you."

"You have me," he murmured, sliding first one finger and then another into her, nearly losing it at the unbelievable perfection of her body. She was tight, hot, her muscles clenching in a rhythm he could feel resonating all the way through him.

Suddenly he knew he couldn't take it anymore. Rolling onto his back, he reached into the nightstand by Sophie's bed and pulled out a condom. After rolling it on quickly, he pulled Sophie over him and, with his hands on her hips, gently guided her onto him.

She cried out as he sank into her, arched her back and clutched at his hands until he twined his fingers with hers. Something about that connection, that joining of Sophie's hands with his own as she rode him, sent him right up to the edge of his control.

Fighting to hang on, never wanting the feelings to end—never wanting the closeness between them to dissipate—he clung to sanity even as her breath grew quicker and her movements more frantic. He reveled in the feel of her around him, rejoiced in the slight pressure of her warm weight on his stomach as she slowly moved herself over him.

"Jack," she moaned breathlessly and he knew it was a plea, knew she was close to shattering again. And he loved it. How could he not when he was the one benefitting from her glorious, unselfish passion?

Slipping his hands around her hips, he cupped her gorgeous, round ass in his hands. She gasped, arched, but she didn't deny him and as he slid his finger inside of her, he whispered, "Let it take you, my sweet Sophie. Let it have you."

And she did, her back arching above him like a bow as the waves exploded through her. Her sex clenched around him again and again, pulling him deeper. Taking him home.

At the last minute she leaned down and brushed her lips over his as her gorgeous green eyes looked deep into his own. That was all it took, those moments of connection so deep and profound that he couldn't help feeling like they would be tangled together forever.

With a moan, he let himself go, and the release

that swept through him was so strong, so powerful, that for a moment it was like death itself.

"I love you, Sophie," he said as the orgasm swamped him. "I love you."

"I love you, too," she whispered in his ear.

And that's when he knew. No matter what had happened in their pasts, no matter what happened in their future, he and Sophie and the boys would face it together.

* * * * *

HEART & HOME

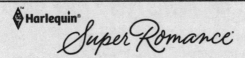

COMING NEXT MONTH
AVAILABLE JUNE 12, 2012

#1782 UNRAVELING THE PAST
The Truth about the Sullivans
Beth Andrews

#1783 UNEXPECTED FAMILY
Molly O'Keefe

#1784 BRING HIM HOME
Karina Bliss

#1785 THE ONLY MAN FOR HER
Delta Secrets
Kristi Gold

#1786 NAVY RULES
Whidbey Island
Geri Krotow

#1787 A LIFE REBUILT
The MacAllisters
Jean Brashear

REQUEST YOUR FREE BOOKS!
2 FREE NOVELS PLUS 2 FREE GIFTS!

Harlequin

Super Romance

Exciting, emotional, unexpected!

YES! Please send me 2 FREE Harlequin® Superromance® novels and my 2 FREE gifts (gifts are worth about $10). After receiving them, if I don't wish to receive any more books, I can return the shipping statement marked "cancel." If I don't cancel, I will receive 6 brand-new novels every month and be billed just $4.69 per book in the U.S. or $5.24 per book in Canada. That's a saving of at least 15% off the cover price! It's quite a bargain! Shipping and handling is just 50¢ per book in the U.S. and 75¢ per book in Canada.* I understand that accepting the 2 free books and gifts places me under no obligation to buy anything. I can always return a shipment and cancel at any time. Even if I never buy another book, the two free books and gifts are mine to keep forever.

135/336 HDN FC6T

Name	(PLEASE PRINT)	
Address		Apt. #
City	State/Prov.	Zip/Postal Code

Signature (if under 18, a parent or guardian must sign)

Mail to the Reader Service:
IN U.S.A.: P.O. Box 1867, Buffalo, NY 14240-1867
IN CANADA: P.O. Box 609, Fort Erie, Ontario L2A 5X3

Not valid for current subscribers to Harlequin Superromance books.
Are you a current subscriber to Harlequin Superromance books and want to receive the larger-print edition?
Call **1-800-873-8635** or visit www.ReaderService.com.

* Terms and prices subject to change without notice. Prices do not include applicable taxes. Sales tax applicable in N.Y. Canadian residents will be charged applicable taxes. Offer not valid in Quebec. This offer is limited to one order per household. All orders subject to credit approval. Credit or debit balances in a customer's account(s) may be offset by any other outstanding balance owed by or to the customer. Please allow 4 to 6 weeks for delivery. Offer available while quantities last.

Your Privacy—The Reader Service is committed to protecting your privacy. Our Privacy Policy is available online at www.ReaderService.com or upon request from the Reader Service.

We make a portion of our mailing list available to reputable third parties that offer products we believe may interest you. If you prefer that we not exchange your name with third parties, or if you wish to clarify or modify your communication preferences, please visit us at www.ReaderService.com/consumerchoice or write to us at Reader Service Preference Service, P.O. Box 9062, Buffalo, NY 14269. Include your complete name and address.

HSR11

Harlequin®

SPECIAL EDITION

Life, Love and Family

USA TODAY bestselling author

Marie Ferrarella

enchants readers in

ONCE UPON A MATCHMAKER

Micah Muldare's aunt is worried that her nephew is going to wind up alone in his old age...but this matchmaking mama has just the thing! When Micah finds himself accused of theft, defense lawyer Tracy Ryan agrees to help him as a favor to his aunt, but soon finds herself drawn to more than just his case. Will Micah open up his heart and realize Tracy is his match?

Available June 2012

Saddle up with Harlequin® series books this summer and find a cowboy for every mood!

Available wherever books are sold.

www.Harlequin.com

HSE65674

A grim discovery is about to change everything for Detective Layne Sullivan—including how she interacts with her boss!

Read on for an exciting excerpt of the upcoming book UNRAVELING THE PAST by Beth Andrews....

SOMETHING WAS UP—otherwise why would Chief Ross Taylor summon her back out? As Detective Layne Sullivan walked over, she grudgingly admitted he was doing well. But that didn't change the fact that the Chief position should have been hers.

Taylor turned as she approached. "Detective Sullivan, we have a situation."

"What's the problem?"

He aimed his flashlight at the ground. The beam illuminated a dirt-encrusted skull.

"Definitely a problem." And not something she'd expected. Not here. "How'd you see it?"

"Jess stumbled upon it looking for her phone."

Layne looked to where his niece huddled on a log. "I'll contact the forensics lab."

"Already have a team on the way. I've also called in units to search for the rest of the remains."

So he'd started the ball rolling. Then, she'd assume command while he took Jess home. "I have this under control."

Though it was late, he was clean shaven and neat, his flat stomach a testament to his refusal to indulge in doughnuts. His dark blond hair was clipped at the sides, the top long enough to curl.

The female part of Layne admitted he was attractive.

The cop in her resented the hell out of him for it.

"You get a lot of missing-persons cases here?" he asked.

"People don't go missing from Mystic Point." Although plenty of them left. "But we have our share of crime."

"I'll take the lead on this one."

Bad enough he'd come to *her* town and taken the position she was meant to have, now he wanted to mess with *how* she did her job? "Why? I'm the only detective on third shift and your second in command."

"Careful, Detective, or you might overstep."

But she'd never played it safe.

"I don't think it's overstepping to clear the air. You have something against me?"

"I assign cases based on experience and expertise. You don't have to like how I do that, but if you need to question every decision, perhaps you'd be happier somewhere else."

"Are you threatening my job?"

He moved so close she could feel the warmth from his body. "I'm not threatening anything." His breath caressed her cheek. "I'm giving you the choice of what happens next."

What will Layne choose? Find out in
UNRAVELING THE PAST by Beth Andrews,
available June 2012 from Harlequin® Superromance®.

And be sure to look for the other two books
in Beth's THE TRUTH ABOUT THE SULLIVANS series
available in August and October 2012.

HSREXP0612

Harlequin Romance

A touching new duet from fan-favorite author

SUSAN MEIER

First Time
DADS!

When millionaire CEO Max Montgomery spots
Kate Hunter-Montgomery—the wife he's never forgotten—
back in town with a daughter who looks just like him, he's
determined to win her back. But can this savvy business tycoon
convince Kate to trust him a second time with her heart?

Find out this June in

THE TYCOON'S SECRET DAUGHTER

And look for book 2 coming this August!

NANNY FOR THE MILLIONAIRE'S TWINS

Saddle up with Harlequin® series books this summer
and find a cowboy for every mood!

THREAT OF DARKNESS

VALERIE HANSEN

As a nurse and special advocate for children, Samantha Rochard is used to danger in her small town of Serenity, Arkansas. But when she suspects a little boy is in jeopardy, she puts herself in the line of fire...and her only source of protection is old flame and police officer John Waltham. Can they team up again in time to save this child's life?

THE DEFENDERS

Available June 2012 wherever books are sold.

**Look for a special bonus book in each
Love Inspired® Suspense book in June.**